1

To all of as

Stefania Scialabba

I wanted HER

Love is complicated for everyone,
let alone between women.

"Cut the pack."

The air is cold even for November, but the fortune teller, seated comfortably at her little table under one of the archways that line some of the streets of Turin, doesn't seem to notice. Wrapped in her green coat and with a hairpiece clipped to the nape of her neck, she stares at me with young eyes in a wrinkled face. Everything about her exudes mystery and you can tell that she comes from old money, all of which is long gone.

Elegant posture, a big ring with an opaque yellow stone and beautifully made but old and worn clothes, that she insists on wearing as a final ostentation of the difference between her world and that of online shopping.

"Cut the pack" she repeats, visibly irritated.

"Concentrate".

Her firm, deep voice rings out direct and clear amidst the chaos, as if the noise of the Saturday afternoon traffic and shoppers all around us simply aren't there. She looks at me and I'm captivated, hypnotised, as if we were inside a room, a shamanic hut, or in the middle of the desert, instead of standing outside a patisserie shop in the city centre.

And at this very moment I understand how she has managed to get me to pay her sixty euros for a general card reading and the chance to ask one specific question.

As I watch her, fighting with myself and against the feeling that I'm about to faint from standing in the same position for so long, I finally split the pack of Tarot cards. I can just imagine the scene: a crowd of people gathered around my momentarily unconscious body lying on the ground, and the fortune teller disappearing quickly around the corner to avoid being accused of anything.

I swallow a nervous giggle and take a breath to say something, while the grumpy fortune teller stares at the cards on the camping table in front of her.

Angelica.

It could be the name of a woman who sells candles or angel caller bells, one of those people who give off a sense of calm as you look at them, convincing you to buy a useless little chime that is only going to gather dust and which, every time you move house, will turn up in a drawer or a jewellery box and be packed up again. As if it were a treasure, lost among the things you forget about after hurriedly emptying your pockets. Something you bought because you needed to feel that you were taking home a little piece of the light you saw that day in the woman you bought it from.

But her eyes hold no trace of sharing and no trace of light, just cynical energy crystallised in the iciness of the truth that she unveils as she glances at the cards.

And you end up believing everything she says.

Since she isn't going to be telling you anything nice, you are absolutely convinced that she's really a witch who, having fallen on hard times, has decided to abandon her cauldron and tell people their future instead.

"It's a bit cold to be working outdoors".

I say something just to break the silence and ease the embarrassment that fills the air. I begin to smile but the smile literally dies on my face when, without even lifting her head, Angelica raises her hand, palm facing towards me, and snaps her fingers shut in the shape of a beak, basically telling me to shut up and listen without saying a word. I find her attitude too bewitching and entertaining to be annoyed, so I simply stand there in silence and wait patiently for an answer. She lights another cigarette while the smoke from the butt of the one before is still rising from the jam jar lid ashtray on the table. She keeps on moving the cards spread out in front of her, seeming to have forgotten that I'm there at all, and mumbles constantly under her breath, without me being able to make out a word she says. There's no mistaking the scolding tone of her voice though. She's probably telling me off because I'm not paying sufficient attention to the cosmic powers that are going out of their way to reveal interpretations of my past and predictions of my future.

"I can't remember your name." she says, waiting for an answer and never raising her eyes from the cards.

"Of course you can't remember it because I haven't told you." Just for a moment, I toy with the idea of making her guess it, but the motionless insistence conveyed by her silence convinces me it isn't a good idea. "My name's Sonia."

"It seems you've lost control of a lot of things over the last year". She slowly raises her head and looks curiously at me, mixing up the few not particularly clear ideas I've accumulated over the years with regard to Tarot card readings.

Shouldn't I be the one to be looking curious and waiting for answers? While I'm still wondering, I hear her say: "tell me about it".

This strange woman has a capacity to verbally condense things which is directly proportionate to the descriptive power evoked by her tone of voice and, despite the interest that her behaviour continues to arouse in me, I lean gently forward onto the table and, smiling ironically, answer:

"you tell me".

She puts out the cigarette, hitting the centre of the jam jar lid without even looking at it, her eyes still staring into mine with embarrassing insistence. Like a slow-motion replay, her face seems to grow slowly bigger, moving closer and closer to me, so that I can catch the deepest but most impenetrable light of her irritation at my cocky reply.

"The cards reveal everything but they have to be interpreted and if you talk to me, I can find the truth".

With all my haughty arrogance, I shove my hands into my coat pockets and shrug my shoulders.

"It's my own fault for spending all that money on a game, but you could at least have told me something to justify all the paraphernalia and air of mystery. I mean people pay you to create a few illusions. But I know what you're doing".

I don't even expect an answer because I've already paid her, so I just nod my goodbye. With something halfway between a cough and a bored sigh, she looks at me and says: "Give me a cigarette and a light." And as I hold the lighter towards her, she continues: "when she died you thought you'd be free, but nothing's changed at all, has it?" Angelica is one of the few women who can say that they've left me open-mouthed.

2

She was dead.

Both my sister and I had been convinced that she would have buried us all or that her constant, cyclical suicide threats would have made someone lose their patience and murder her to put an end to her pathetic wailing.

But no.

After years of smoking cigarettes as if they were good for her instead of cancer sticks, along with her occasional abuse of antidepressants, coupled with the most appalling use of a car that she should have been banned from owning never mind driving, my mother had died a stupid, random death that had taken her away during one of the things she did all the time.

Ready to go out dancing, and dressed like a prostitute, she had slipped in her heels and broken her neck. That was the last photograph of her life.

There she was, lifeless, on the kitchen floor, still holding the cigarette butt, which had burnt her finger. Embarrassed by so much chaos and all the condolences, my sister and I let the neighbours and the police think that our awkward silence was caused by the pain of our loss, just to avoid having to explain that the whole thing really didn't bother us at all.

Who were we supposed to call? Was there anyone who might be interested in her accident? How had they managed to trace us?

One of her neighbours stared suspiciously at us: "Are you her daughters? I've never seen you before."

Before I could drum up a diplomatic answer which wouldn't trigger a reaction, my sister summed everything up perfectly. "Yes, we're her daughters, unfortunately, but now it's over."

A deathly silence that had nothing to do with the woman lying dead on the floor filled the kitchen, possibly the building and maybe even the entire street. Shocked, accusing glances alternated with those of the neighbours who thought they hadn't fully understood. An atomic mushroom cloud of astonished silence stopped them from breathing. Emma turned to face me, smirking as she tried her best not to laugh, and I dropped my gaze quickly to avoid looking at her. I was almost convinced that my mother was finding the situation just as funny. After all, she was the one who had taught us to laugh when things got gruesome. Not because she had a particularly ironic sense of humour but simply because she would regularly get herself into some kind of mess and then blame someone else, twisting the facts until she found a way and a reason to laugh about it all.

Anyway, it really was over. Yet somehow, it didn't feel as though her hatred had died with her.

The shrill sound of the zip on the body bag they were putting her into dragged me back to reality, along with the heavy scent of her perfume, which she'd evidently doused herself in before falling off her four-inch heels.

Considering the bitterness I felt, my inner journey towards acceptance and practice of Buddhism obviously weren't really working. I probably needed to go back and repeat a few steps.

The last thing I remember, and which will always come to mind when I think about the day my mother died, is the hand of the policeman giving me the keys to the house. That and the neighbours telling me that she owed about six months' rent, my sister's face, which looked like she wanted to drop another bomb, and my half-stifled giggle, which always reminds me just how much like my mother I am. Apart from her four-inch heels, her perfume and, from that day on, her broken neck.

The preparations for the funeral were taken care of with a phone call to a friend who had inherited her father's passion for funeral services and, after a long succession of entrepreneurial disasters, had discovered that burying bodies was her life's mission.

She was going to see to everything as quickly and as cheaply as possible.

For various reasons, my mother was going to be cremated, and the fact that it was what she had wanted wasn't top of the list. Basically, we wanted to lock her inside an urn and wall her up in a concrete burial cell. Hidden away safely like the Jumanji box to make sure that not even the tiniest bit of her remains could filter into the ground.

"Telegram!"

The postman shouted so loudly through the intercom that I could have heard him even without picking up the receiver. "Telegram?" I said, facing Emma, whose bored reply was "do people still send those things?"

"Sorry for your loss, condolences to the whole family".

Cousins twenty-four times removed whose names I didn't even know sorrowfully send telegram conveying condolences to family who couldn't care less. "Do you have to answer a telegram?" Emma looked at me and, in all seriousness, said: "Google it."

And so we discovered that funeral etiquette dictates that you send out mourning cards a couple of months after the funeral, with a couple of strictly hand-written lines of thanks.

3

Too proud to let Angelica see that she has surprised me, I stare into her eyes, shut my mouth and smile. Nevertheless, I get the distinct feeling that the expression in my eyes is failing to obey my brain and is screaming out all the chaotic thoughts that are running around in my head.
We're all witches and wizards in the end. At least according to the new current developed from an offshoot of Neuro Linguistic Programming which - having metabolised the

decline in sales of life coaching books - has gradually changed the description in their prefaces, but without changing the guru of reference and attributing quantum properties to one simple reality: anything is possible if you want it badly enough. At the end of the day, that's all there is to it.

The most powerful magic, the most complex spell and the most successful motivation always stem from your energy and from that stupid but powerful organ that is your brain. So part of me continues interacting with Angelica while the other looks for a logical and scientifically esoteric explanation for the precision of her intuition. Her statement has floored me so I have to find something in my attitude that has given her the clues she needed to make it.

While all these proud thoughts, which are anything but open to the acceptance of the existence of someone who, with their icy but penetrating gaze, is able to glean information from some ordinary cards purchased from a flea market, not only on my life but also on my innermost thoughts and feelings, run through my head, Angelica keeps on scanning my soul with her investigative clairvoyance.

"The choices in your life are all feminine. You're surrounded by women and they all play a different role, but you never let any of them get close". And now there's a glimmer of a smile on her lips, because the crafty old witch knows that she's found the seam of gold in the mine that I've just opened up to her, showing her the way and the path to take.

Calm down.

It's obvious that, if she can read my mind, then I can deviate the things she sees. Mindful of the energy therapy, Reiki and shamanism courses attended with various cultural associations, I try to implement concepts that I'd always thought useless in my everyday life until now. My grandad, with that presumptuousness that I've inherited from him, used to say that "when you read something that seems stupid and pointless, keep going anyway, until you get to the end, and you'll see that, at some point in your life, you'll be able to use it to your advantage. And he was right. I never thought that attending courses on esoterism was pointless but nor had I ever taken into consideration the possibility of applying the things I learned to my everyday life! Every day?

But then how many people would ever dream of having their cards read in the middle of the day in front of a cake shop in the city centre by a doubtful looking fortune teller? Should I see it as a sign to be read in an esoteric key or in a psychiatric key? Or, as my sister would say, should I see a neurologist to rule out the possibility that I have a brain tumour which causes completely incomprehensible attitudes and alters my interpretation of events? "Do you want to know what the cards say or are you too busy minding your own business? I haven't got all day!" Scolded once again by the fortune teller, I concentrate and answer her question, which isn't really a question at all. Oh but she's clever!

"You're right. I don't let anyone, men or women, get close". And as I say the words, I imagine myself inside a bubble of hot, protective light which doesn't let anything I don't want inside, remembering it from the various courses I've taken part in. And now I feel even more stupid, because it was me that wanted to stop in front of that odd-looking woman and ask her some questions. The bubble slowly deflates, dissolving into lots of pretty beams of light, as though my subconscious and my energy are happy not to have to concentrate on something so unimportant. But it IS important. When someone rational and critical decides, of their own free will, to venture into the oblivion of illusion, it's a bit like seeing a Nobel prize-winner suddenly start watching reality shows on TV, taking a real interest in them with no critical spirit whatsoever. It's a noteworthy anthropological event which has to be seconded to understand where it's going to lead. So I decide to stop fighting, keep my wits about me, and let the cards tell me things about my life which, probably distracted by circumstance, I've missed. It's easy to concentrate on a tiny detail while it's happening and then fail to consider something immense as it touches you. So why not give that dusty chime discovered by accident, attracting my attention with its noisy, tuneless tinkling, a chance?

4

"Passion Fruit. What a great nick! Where are you writing from?" Those were the days of chat rooms. You joined with the excuse of shared interests and the hope of meeting someone interesting. I was twenty-three at the time. I had only just realised who I was but had still to fully accept myself. They were the days of my first clumsy experiments and early adult emotions, accompanied by new hormones and an awareness that was still a little childish.

Ada was younger than me, seemingly smarter and with a greater desire to shock, first herself and then everyone else. It didn't matter who and how. The important thing was to experiment because, at the dawning of a technological age that was just around the corner, the future pioneers of the social networks, surfers infected by the humming of the modem as it made a connection and reassured them with its sound, were convinced that they were protected by their anonymity, hidden behind a screen, and excited by the interest that it could generate.

That evening I'd stayed behind at work. It wasn't so much that I didn't want to go home. I really wanted to get on with a job that I was working on and, although I carried on working, chatting to strangers made the fact that it was well after 10 p.m. seem less important. And then there was her.

Answering elegantly with feigned disinterest, and with a command of the Italian language that was almost moving compared to the level of most of the other people online, she revealed no anxious need to win you over or fear that you might suddenly disappear. The perfectly timed pauses a woman would know how to use on a date, separated by intense looks and ramblings of the soul. She managed to make me feel as though I was sitting at the table of a restaurant with a bottle of wine, music playing softly in the background, completely caught up in the light of her eyes and the movement of her lips. It was a real feat of dialectics considering that I was simply seated on a swivel chair at the desk in my empty studio, staring at a computer screen.

Ada dreamed about everything and talked about nothing, creating fabulous mental images alternated with sharp expressions of annoyance, when I hesitated to answer her or caused by an unwelcome digression. Slowly, but a slowness perceived only on the inside, curiosity began to wind its way through parts of me I didn't even know existed and the conversation lasted all night long, leaving us wanting just one thing. Each of us yearned to hear the other's voice. Even before seeing what we looked like, which we first discovered on screen, we needed to bridge the distance that had born witness to and caused such a violent and sudden attraction.

Sustained by the written illusion of our emotions, the meeting of our voices had merged immediately into a sort of pact between twin souls, thirsty and unable to avoid probing, subject by subject, all of our *raisons d'être,* to the point where meeting and loving each other didn't only seem natural but was a need that was impossible to control.

Just like in the best romantic films, our first meeting was at the railway station. We had sent each other pictures after declaring our love for one another, even before we'd smelled each other's scent. Neither of us said anything about the photo received. As if talking about the outer shell of the soul were almost an insult. As if we didn't want to assign importance to the first blackspot on the vision created in our minds.

"The Intercity train from Venezia Mestre to Torino Porta Nuova is arriving at platform 15". The metallic computerised voice made a standard announcement, wrapped in anxiety and anticipation, the result of a day filled with expectation and hours spent in front of the wardrobe trying to find something to wear that would say everything about me, dressing me up in irresistibility and everything that the long phone calls had said about me.

Standing strategically behind one of the columns in the station, I waited for the girl I'd shared part of my inner self and so many of my desires with to arrive, so that I could catch a glimpse of her before she saw me, gaining a sort of advantage.

And there she was: a red blouse with a plunging neckline revealing incredibly generous breasts, and faded bellbottom jeans with frayed hems that shielded a pair of flip-flops. Short hair and a brazen expression, seeking out her prey.

In spite of all the sentimental recognitions that my impatient heart had skipped before beating wildly for a conversation that lived up to my mental expectations, my first thought had been a horrified judgement of the choice of flip-flops, a red blouse which left her back completely bare and a black lace bra that was clearly visible, depriving her of all sensuality and displaying a heavy dose of bad taste. At that point, I was greedy for her eyes. I needed to be sure that I hadn't been mistaken and wasn't going to have to admit that I'd put myself in an embarrassing situation with a stranger whose spirit I'd dressed up as kindred to mine merely in my imagination.

The strange sensation wouldn't go away. The awkward greeting, kisses on the cheek like two strangers who feel obliged to hug each other but don't know why, and the walk towards the exit, body heading in the right direction and subconscious seeking every possible escape route, hoping for the arrival of an emergency phone call or a natural disaster. Neither happened of course. When we got to my car, we put her backpack - emptied of schoolbooks and filled with her clothes, which had the job of creating a sense of anticipation and of cloaking her in her previous conversations - and then found ourselves seated inside, face to face.

Eyes gazing into eyes, I began with an intense "I love you anyway". And in that very moment, flip-flops, blouse and slutty bra lost all importance and the nights spent in her company on the phone, imagining her smiles and her expressions, took shape in an embrace which I now know we both needed. With that statement we had sealed a pact made across the miles and ignored the implications of the word "anyway", which tasted a bit like "even though you look like this."

Everything in my life had always been dictated by a convulsive rhythmic change that went from calm routine to absolute chaos without anything in between. No warning and no preparation.

In exactly the same way that my anger management technique has always been based on putting up with things until I explode, I've always waited until things in my life have been so unbearable that I can't cope any longer before upending my false stability and that of whoever's involved with me. What was often swapped for a patient attitude so marked as to be taken for zen philosophy was nothing more than a constant deaf and dumb seething that fermented until it obscured all reason and intent. Once the hurricane of change was over, all we could do was survey the wreckage.

We had already decided to book a room in a hotel not far from my house so that we had a sort of emergency exit from a situation the evolution of which neither of us were sure of.

I kept watching Ada who, with a wilfully relaxed expression, awaited our arrival at the hotel.

It was all very strained. Ada's tone of voice seemed to hide more of a touch of curiosity than a show of tolerance.

"Hi Rita, what is it?"

"I can't find the shots you left for Roberto's client." She affected a professional air, having found the perfect excuse for a bit of investigation.

"I thought I told you. I gave Roberto the file myself yesterday afternoon."

"Sorry, I must have forgotten" followed by the shortest of pauses and then, all in one breath: "what are you doing today? Are you coming back to work?"

"No Rita, I'm not coming back."

During our phone conversation, Ada continued stroking my hand, working her way up my arm to my neck, watching me all the time. Rita was still on the phone when we pulled up outside the hotel but I wasn't listening to a single word she was saying. I followed Ada to the entrance, staring at her back, all thoughts of her blouse and bra long forgotten. Along with Rita.

The call came to an abrupt end between checking in at the hotel reception and reaching our room. Ada laughed, satisfied at the idea of being the cause of a mini drama, while the woman who had accompanied us to the room stared at us enquiringly. The room was plain but clean and, once we were alone with nothing to distract us, a very embarrassing silence began to fill the air.

"I have to take a shower. My skin smells of train." Ada stared at me with a dark and penetrating gaze that seemed to be waiting for something to light it up.

"Go on then. I'll come back later if you like and take you out somewhere." I'd said it smiling. We were playing with each other, in the same way that we'd played on the phone for the last few weeks. A verbal sparring match that I'd decided I was going to win. The excitement was tangible, understandably, because the virtual foreplay had last forever, between hot telephone calls and even hotter messages.

I got the feeling she wanted me to try and kiss her so that she could push me away, or at least pretend to. An immature but feminine dance as old as the world and incredibly chauvinistic, especially when acted out between women. It was as though we were performing a sadly seductive screenplay stolen from a romantic film in which the bold young man roughly grabs the girl, while she fights him off without really convincing anyone, before giving in with a sigh that's somewhere between resignation and pleasant surprise.

In this case it was obvious that Ada thought I should be impersonating some version or other of the bold young man, but I couldn't have been more different. "The choice is yours."

Ada lay down on the bed and, looking bored, pointed to the TV. "Can you pass me the remote please? I'll put some music on."

Casually unbuttoning her blouse, she drew one of the pillows towards her stomach and then lay face-down on top of it, in the position typical of children getting ready to watch cartoons. It wasn't openly seductive but there was a powerful contrast between her expression and her body language. A little Lolita playing at ensnaring me. She was just two years my junior but already seemed to have a sensuality that, while being new-born, was, nevertheless, explosive. The TV was on and the remote was on the bed next to Ada, who finally gave in. "Kiss me, please, I can't wait any more. To hell with the shower". Sex between two people who've shared the deepest, most intimate thoughts but with no physical contact, none of the smells and none of the glances. Something completely unknown surrounded by an absolute lack of knowledge. Ada had sold herself as a woman of many talents, yet at that moment, as we undressed urgently, the truth revealed her for what she was; an embarrassed young woman amazed by the pleasure she felt and shyly gave. The effect was immediate, galvanised by the feeling that all teachers must experience in front of a class of promising students. We spent several intense hours getting to know our bodies and our reactions. Ada held onto me as if she was afraid I would slip out of her grasp and her breath on my face filled me with a whole range of emotions and reactions that were new to me too. Love.

When I had seen her at the station, I had instinctively thought that I was going to be disappointed. Yet the excitement was triggered by what I had initially thought might have been a limit. She was cloaked in false experience and discovering her anxieties, seeing her open her eyes at such unknown pleasure and a genuine desire for more were like a drug. We lay naked in each other's arms until later, before going out in search of food and a place where we could pretend we had some kind of social rapport above the sheets. Ada decided to flirt with everyone in order to try and re-establish a supremacy that she obviously thought she'd lost in bed. I pretended I wasn't interested because I could tell she was doing it on purpose. If we'd both been smarter, we would have realised that this wasn't a good foundation for the relationship that was beginning to take shape.

. . . .

She was crying so desperately that I actually began to think that I'd died and that my spirit was witnessing her being torn apart by the consequent pain, tied to the earthly dimension not only by incredible bad luck but also by the thread of her theatrical lament. All I had done was tell her I was in love with Ada. I hadn't even thought about mentioning beforehand that I was homosexual for two precise reasons: firstly, because I'd already told her when we had been on holiday two years before, although my words had merely been chewed up, digested and expelled during the ten-day silence that ensued.

The second reason was that, throughout my childhood and adolescence, I had done nothing other than fall in love with women, beginning with my paediatrician and ending with Madonna, with various schoolfriends and neighbours in between.

Yet my mother, faced with the facts in flesh, blood and flip-flops, had only been able to stage a colossal tragedy, involving friends and family who, far from being surprised, advised her not to worry about it, telling her that they had already known for some time. Their words only enhanced her compulsive need to suffer for something, obliging the whole family to observe a mournful attitude whenever anyone else was around. The fact was that the corpse absolutely refused to be dead or even sad for that matter, and I set about sharing my incredible happiness without a care in the world.

"Of course I'm in no position to tell you how to live your life but you're definitely not bringing anyone here. You can find yourself somewhere else to live, close by, so you can do what you want but still give me a hand." She had said it with an expression of forced tolerance, as though it were an inevitable but unfair compromise that she was prepared to make for the greater good.

Perhaps my existence depended on that statement which, in its complete absurdity, had finally given me the courage to box up all my books and camera and set off, after handing in my notice at work, for the city where Ada had chosen to go to University and where I had chosen to find out who I was.

Love has the flavour of omnipotence when a relationship with another person makes us fall in love with ourselves.

. . . .

Far away from home, from my sister and beloved cat, I walked around town hand in hand with Ada, in places that were new, always wanting to discover something more, together with all the emotions and lessons they were teaching us. We each fed off the eyes of the other, completely unable to avoid spending every minute of our existence together.

We lived in a residential area near the centre of Parma, a university city so different from the life I was used to in Turin that I sometimes felt as though I'd moved in terms of time and space and not just geographically. It wasn't long before the days of amazement and curiosity came to an end and we were left with the task of adapting to our new life before the detachment from everything we'd been used to before caused us to collapse into a state of melancholy depression. Fortunately, the fact that we were living together made everything new and this was enough to distract us from everything else. Even looking for a new job. And the switch from the Lira to the Euro passed by almost unnoticed.

We had fun commenting on how the combined use of the two currencies resulted in an arbitrary interpretation of how to calculate the right change in the various shops.

Very often, people who go through moments of historical change really haven't the slightest idea of their importance. Between smiles and lovers' tiffs, our first months of life together settled into a routine that left no room for contact with reality.

I had found work in a pub. When I had left Turin, I had left behind a job as a photographer in an advertising studio, and then found myself making sandwiches in Parma.

"But what am I supposed to do when you're at work in the evening?" She was annoyed and in a dreadful mood as I got ready to go out. "You could go out with your friends and then come and meet me after work so we can go for a drink together". I felt the chill hit the air even before her anger exploded.

"So you don't care?"

Happiness is a matter of personal satisfaction but, at that time, my smiles all depended on Ada's smiles. "Of course I care but I can't expect you to sit around the house doing nothing while you wait for me." I put my arms around her, kissing her neck, and lowered my voice "Or we could both stay here and go to bed. I'll find a job with better hours". Her smile sealed it.

The supremacy that had been established the first time we'd gone to that hotel together had soon become a sort of addiction. Ada did everything she could to goad me, with a view to receiving pleasure that would never be returned in full, promising that one day she would give herself to me completely if I succeeded in winning her trust and her heart, and if I could find the key to open up the door to all the things she kept hidden away. All it took was a second for her to hold all the power. The days went by to the pace of an inner rhythm that merely reinforced the impression that I had gone to live in one of those glass snow globes that come to life when you shake them. But the only time I came to life was when I was with Ada. I had forgotten about me, and my mother and sister had forgotten about me too. No phone calls and no visits. Just a single message from Emma in the whole year, as if the simple fact that I had moved away meant that I no longer existed. I was alone and in love with Ada, with the awareness that I had always been the only one to make any effort at all in relationships that had become frozen when I'd stopped doing anything to fuel them. Sometimes you have to step away from your life and look at it from the outside to understand the mechanics.

But realising something doesn't automatically put an end to it.

The only plans that attracted mine and Ada's attention, and to which we dedicated any time, involved being together. And that's why, at the end of the year, we decided to move. The time had come for me to find a real job, that would allow me to keep myself, and Ada, having failed to take even a single exam, had decided to change faculty.

So, about a year after our first enthusiastic move, I found myself moving again, this time with the feeling that I'd lost the personal motivation I'd had the first time around. This time I felt as though I was betraying myself and I didn't even know why.

Despite my feelings for Ada, something was telling me that, not just for myself but for our relationship too, I should take a different path.

But instead, I packed up my books again and decided not to focus on my gut instinct, believing that it was a sensation dictated by fear that was attempting to make me change my mind. The tingling sensation behind my back, on the other hand, which was pushing me in a different direction, was perhaps a breath of courage that urged me not to lose myself in decisions that seemed obvious, but to follow my heart. That choice marked the future of our relationship, although we didn't realise it until three years later.

5

Those feelings we can't quite identify live in and fee
thoughts, swinging backwards and forwards in a mer
which we purposely keep hidden away.

How many situations have we sworn we wouldn't end up in
again and how many situations have we lapsed right back into
without even realising it?

What are the mechanisms that influence our decisions, making
us compulsively repeat the same mistakes time after time, even
when we think we've understood and won't make them again?

Our brain hides most of itself inside a box protected against
paths it knows and believes it has to repeat because it's a lazy
coward that forces us to keep going around in circles rather
than waste energy seeking out a new road. Lost in these
thoughts, I realise that it's cold and someone's staring intensely
at me.

"They're just tarot cards. If you have to wander off on a
shamanic journey into your memories and ask questions about
your life every time I turn a card, you'd be better off seeing a
psychologist. And it would be cheaper." Angelica.

Arms folded with a satisfied smile on her face, she continues
mixing the cards, nodding at me to indicate a stool hidden
under her camping table transformed into a divination studio. I
glance uncertainly around. Standing in front of a card reader is
very different from sitting comfortably at a table. My body acts
faster than my doubts and, while my head is still weighing up
the pros and cons, I sit down opposite this strange woman.

"Like everyone else, you're here to have your life revealed to
you in a way that you can understand. Making sense of our
actions strips us of the responsibility for having performed

them. But choices made in the past are always clearer and more numerous when we see them through the cards. Now that your first memory has come to mind, you know exactly what you should have done."

"Everyone seems to think that it's easy to see a situation after the event. You'd be surprised dear Angelica, but it's not like that for me. I'd still do everything in exactly the same way and take exactly the same path today, taking care not to change a single thing."

I study her face, hoping to see even the slightest sign of surprise but I think that her habit of being mysterious and unreadable must have caused some sort of physiognomic paralysis that prevents her from expressing anything that isn't typical of the perfect fortune teller.

"If you don't want to change even the slightest detail you must be happy with your life the way it is or have achieved something you're afraid of losing".

Now it's my turn to smile. "I'm pleased with what I've learned along the way and yes, I've found something I don't ever want to run the risk of losing."

Thoughtful, or at least apparently so, she places the pack of cards in the middle of the table and, with a bored gesture, invites me to cut it. Once again, I have to concentrate on the question and, once again, a whole series of questions come flooding into my mind together, battling for first place. A bit like cars which, approaching a narrowing in the road, instead of slotting neatly into line, all try to push their way through at the same time. Angelica's hand rests firmly on mine and, looking into my eyes, she says: "Concentrate. It's not every day you get the chance to relive certain sentiments. People come to me for answers about the future. You are here to make peace with your past and now I'm curious to find out why."

Do I really have to forgive my past?

Or, by reading the cards, do I want to gain a better understanding of myself to make sure that I'm not just travelling down another reserved lane chosen by my subconscious? I watch her, smiling, and, as I cut the pack, I hear myself murmur: "I like your explanation for this journey! Let's see where it takes us."

The passers-by look on curiously, alternating judgement with complicity, and as Angelica arranges the cards and gets ready, I'm absolutely certain she's going to ask a question rather than give an answer.

She stares at the cards in silence, as if I'm not there, muttering, bothered by something, and shifting the weight of her body from one side of the chair to the other before finally settling back into her original position. She sighs, as though there's nothing she can do, like she has a sort of negative answer to offer someone who's hoping with all their strength for one that's positive. But the answer isn't an answer; it's a question that stems from something that has already happened and that should hold no surprises.

"Now I understand! You're just arrogant! You're convinced that you know what everyone else is thinking and once you've developed your conviction it becomes the truth, regardless of the other person's denial with words and actions" Once again, she has amazed me.

I start thinking that she really is gifted and my head starts filling up with images linked to her idea about me. She still hasn't given me an answer, but then she hasn't really asked me a question either.

Nevertheless, I find myself having to speak because her expression is holding out a question mark that's almost as huge as my surprise. She hasn't actually asked the question only because she knows that that is exactly what I am expecting her to do.

"It isn't that I'm arrogant. It happens all the time. I notice people's real feelings, intentions and thoughts and I've never been wrong yet. Where I go wrong is that I ignore the evidence and insist on trusting the words and actions of the people in my life. Or who were in my life."

Looking at my watch, I realise that only twenty minutes have gone by since I stopped to talk to Angelica. My movement doesn't escape her and she reverts quickly back to her disagreeable character "Don't worry. It won't take much longer. I've got a serious card reading in half an hour so we'd better getter a move on."

6

It had been more than four years since I had spent New Year's Eve in Turin. It was my first without Ada and, even though our relationship was indissoluble and we continued to be part of each other's lives, despite the fact that it had been me that left her, a slight feeling of sadness was inevitable. I had come back to my hometown with the usual haste and boldness, without even thinking about looking for somewhere to live. So I found myself sleeping on the couch in my mother and sister's kitchen. Everyone was forced to put up with this situation, from my mother to Spino, the cat, who, despite reacting elegantly to my return to the fold, was never going to forgive me for bringing Oscarina, the dog Ada had given me for my birthday. The decision regarding who was going to keep her seemed obvious to both of us for two reasons. First of all, she had told me the most horrific stories about her family; all the pets who had been unfortunate enough to end up in their clutches had died under strange circumstances or had gotten lost while out somewhere or on holiday. Secondly, Ada's desire to live life without any type of compromise and without having to prioritise anything other than sudden and fleeting whims was completely incompatible with a dog. Consequently, the sole custody of Oscarina fitted in perfectly with what was, among other things, the main reason for our breakup. I had been convinced that we were laying the foundations of love, only to find out, after four years of intensely shared life together, that I had been a rock, an important and solid figure to hang onto while she experimented and played at life without having to worry about being on her own.

The signs had been there throughout our relationship but the fact that there was a two-year age gap between us (two years which felt like ten) and that we were both women, had confused our judgement. On a morning no different from any other in the university digs we shared in Bologna, Ada was standing in front of the mirror with a strange light in her eyes. She kept adjusting the neckline of her blouse, which was open, revealing her breasts, and examining first the right and then the left side of her body, paying meticulous attention to her backside. She'd even put on some make-up.

She'd never been an early-bird and was breaking with a long-standing habit of throwing on the first thing she came across in the wardrobe to get through the morning's lectures.

"What have you got this morning?" I asked from our bed, my face still snuggled into the pillow. I've always slept naked, so I was rolled up in the covers and wanted her to come back to bed. It wasn't unusual for her to decide to skip a lecture, because I didn't start work until late in the morning and we had just enough time together. I had found a job in a photography studio and the hours were easy to manage.

"Computer studies". Another change of blouse and consequent bilateral inspection.

"What difference does it make what you wear, babe?" A moment's silence and then the truth came tumbling out. That truth that Ada used to strip you of every possibility to feel angry, because you can't lose your temper with someone who's being totally honest with you. "I've got a thing for the Prof. I can't think about anything else. She isn't what you'd call beautiful but there's something about her and I really think I've got a crush on her." I suddenly felt even more naked than before and, as I got out of bed, I dragged the sheets with me, to cover myself while I found my clothes. It wasn't the first time

I'd found myself in this situation. There'd been the girl on her course, the shop assistant, the woman she met online, the teller at the poll station and the goldsmith who lived in the same town as her mother.

"Is that all you've got to say?" I couldn't help being annoyed and disappointed because it didn't matter how much I loved her, it never seemed to be enough.

Ada began huffing and puffing: "do you really have to make a scene like this every time? You know how I feel! I'm an inquisitive animal and I like playing and flirting. That's all I need. I don't love anyone else but you and I'd never go too far, but you can't expect me to suffocate a part of myself. I like being liked. I love you to death, but you know you aren't my type physically. I told you when we met. You're gorgeous, there's no question about it, but you don't turn the active side of me on."

It was true. A week after our first meeting at the station, we'd confirmed our mutual feelings but also confessed the initial sense of disappointment at the physical impact. At least Ada had. I had merely expressed my doubts about her choice of clothing, but I'd always thought she was beautiful. There had been nothing wrong with my self-esteem until I met her. I'd had plenty of admirers in the past, and still have now, but with Ada, the needle on the scale had plummeted dramatically. It no longer indicated my self-esteem but rather a lack of it, drawing attention constantly to my faults, which became bigger and bigger in my head day after day. "How can you possibly think you've got a crush on your computer studies professor? Have you already started your mating ritual?" She winked at me before saying "Of course darling, you know that no one can resist me."

"I'm not going to Germany without you!" Her face had taken on the typical expression of a child terrorised by the idea of having to do something new. It was only an Erasmus and, as I'd already sent in an application to take part in a photographic reportage that was being held in Madrid at the same time she was going to be in Berlin, the argument was well underway. Ada wasn't prepared to compromise. As far as she was concerned, I should give up the job and my chance to spend time gaining experience abroad to follow her, like a lady-in-waiting, to Germany. The trip was still months away so the discussions came and went without ever reaching a conclusion. Going on holiday seemed a much better idea than fighting so we set off to make our peace on the beaches of Greece. It was a perfect opportunity for a bit of harmless flirting on her part and even more frustration on mine. There were no changes in our life under the sheets. Everything was fine, as long as I kept on wanting her. She only ever wanted me in terms of wanting to be wanted, loved and touched, but it was never a two-way thing. "I find you really attractive and I couldn't bear not feeling you inside me, but I just never feel like being inside you. You just don't excite me that way." Did she really have to keep on repeating it?

More cruel sincerity from her and more stupidity from me. What woman wants to be treated like that by another woman? Why use the word love to describe something that's really just a childish need for guarantees and not a mature relationship? Of course, after an initial moment of desperation, I pulled myself together, and that holiday gave me a chance to prove that someone else found me attractive.

We had met a couple of girls on the beach and made friends. Virna and Serena had been together for six years, before deciding to split up when they'd become more like sisters than lovers. No passion and no momentum.

Only the huge amount of affection they felt for one another.

During dinner one evening, I realised that Ada was staring closely at Virna and looked as though she was about to initiate one of her games of seduction. Instinctively, I decided to make a competition out of it and play my cards too. That evening and the six days that followed turned into one long match that undeniably bolstered Virna's ego and resulted in my crushing victory, which ended up leaving me with an empty feeling caused by the fact that my attitude had delighted Ada, who decided we made the perfect couple.

 Soulmates who flirted with other people for fun but, to whom they'd never give their heart. She wasn't even jealous of me. That day, I realised that she didn't love me and that I would have to make a decision for the good of both of us. I had no choice and the only thing I could do was make sure I was one hundred percent certain. So I set off for Germany with her, sacrificing my job and going to live in a little flat with a hysterical girlfriend and the puppy she'd given me for my birthday three months earlier. Like those straight couples who try mending their broken relationships by having a baby, Ada had decided that a cute little puppy would bring us together. In actual fact, her complete lack of responsibility, along with a dose of selfishness that was well above average, had exactly the opposite effect. In Germany, however, I had the chance to open my mind and meet a colleague from the studio I worked for in Turin, who immediately made me an offer. My work was what kept me afloat. You don't have to translate photographs to understand them and there's no complicated plot to read.

I was happy and excited about this new opportunity, which enabled me to work to commission from Augusto, who found work for us.

Augusto was infatuated with Ada and did nothing to hide it. He wasn't invasive or vulgar and his behaviour was simply the celebration of a woman he knew he couldn't have and with whom he could be himself. He made the same jokes when I was there and was forever inviting us to interesting events. Ada couldn't stand having him around because the fact that he was so obviously attracted to her and did nothing to hide it meant that she couldn't play her usual games.

Ada's exams in Berlin didn't go well and this made her even more moody, and also unusually jealous. It was as if the unexpected personal satisfaction that made my eyes shine cast a shadow over her need to be the centre of attention. She still hadn't found a passion that made her heart race in professional or cultural terms and, in her competitive vision of life as part of a couple, this was completely unacceptable. Only that trip abroad could have taught me the things I learned.

A successful relationship needs more than love and passion to thrive. It needs mutual respect and esteem and, above all, complicity. If there's a touch of healthy competition then so much the better, but if that's the only ingredient, then it ceases to be healthy and the relationship becomes a sort of perpetual agony. Despite the fact that I loved Ada (like a sister or a mother at this point), I could no longer put up with her attitude, and her extremely childish nature made me feel increasingly dissatisfied and irritable. I was smart and determined and, fortunately, I realised, just in time, that sacrificing your own happiness for someone else's has a devastating effect on everyone concerned.

I left her one morning after returning to Italy. I had been trying for months. Even though I'd already made the decision, it's hard to let go of the woman you love and of that part of you she takes with her. That day, she cried like she'd never cried before and screamed with all her strength, even trying, convulsively, to slap me. It all ended up with me holding her tight to stop her from her hurting either me or herself, and with more tears, this time calmer and more painful. Ada's dream had been to grow old with me while she played around with other people, coming to tell me all about her adventures at night in front of the telly, as though I were her confidante. A little unstable and with a desperate need to be loved, but unable to give back and to love in return. Because it hurts too much to tell the woman you love that you can't live without her. It's easier to go to sleep together, pretending that there's nothing special about your relationship. In the weeks that followed, to show me how much she was suffering, she revisited all the women who'd made an appearance in her life in some way; those she'd been attracted to, aroused by or even just vaguely interested in, and took them to bed with meticulous precision, making sure I found out about every single one.

The decision to move back to Turin caused a reaction similar to leaving her all over again. This was the second moment in which Ada revealed how deeply hurt she felt by my need to increase the distance between us, taking away my support and the possibility for her to check whether or not I was sorry that I'd lost her. Her formidable character meant that she read the situation from one side only, without ever realising that it wasn't me that was losing someone. Maybe this is why, about a year after that last physical encounter, spending New Year's Eve without her was tinged with a bitter sweetness made up of the feeling of revenge and the desire for adventure combined with a touch of fear. The fear that loving yourself more than you have loved someone else is actually wrong. The fear that grips every human being is based on the eternal conviction that we have to be half of a couple in order to be happy and that, if you leave a relationship that isn't working properly, you might end up with something even worse or (even more terrifying) nothing at all. The dreadful fear of ending up alone makes us either rush into things or stay where we are.

I dragged my sister Emma out for an evening that was unlikely to be particularly exciting, promising her that we'd have more fun than if we sat on the couch all night in front of the telly, listening to our mother whingeing and moaning, or having to witness her parade around the house for an evening that would probably end with the feeling that we had absolutely nothing to celebrate. And I wanted to celebrate the start of something new, a new me and everything that I had set aside for the past four years. I wasn't getting ready so much for New Year's Eve as for the baptism of my new life.

7

Her seemingly hard, inexpressive face had an extraordinary capacity for expressing and revealing the tiniest details of every emotion she felt in the exact moment that her mood changed. I had already had a chance to appreciate the energy that coursed through this very tall and slender girl who, despite the short blonde hair that was so definitely not one of the physical attributes that I usually find attractive in a woman, possessed a silent, restrained sensuality that gave the impression that it was just waiting to be discovered and conquered. Perhaps it had been this thought that had piqued my curiosity and made me want to follow that bunch of losers on the last night of the year to the club they'd chosen. My sister seemed to find the idea fun, or maybe, since we were already out on the town, she was just pretending so that she wouldn't end up feeling like our New Year's Eve had been a disappointment.

Alina behaved like she was part of the club's staff. While she danced and talked to everyone, her eyes were always wandering around the club, checking out what was going on. It was as though she needed to keep the situation under control, just like she'd done all the time we'd been at the bar where we'd waited until the clock chimed midnight to see in the New Year. Bored by hordes of men with little interest in the female sex, Emma concentrated her efforts on trying to create an opportunity for me to talk to the silently mysterious bartender with the piercing blue eyes. Apparently, she had spent the whole evening trying to catch my eye without me even noticing. "Are you blind? That's the third time she's paraded in front of you holding a glass, staring at you!" Emma laughed and looked around. "Fucking hell, this place is full of men and all they can do is look at each other. They don't even see me!" Emma pointed her finger at me and, displaying something halfway between drunkenness and bitterness said: "You're right in the middle of the perfect hunting ground and you don't even realise you've scored!"

Not that I could really be blamed, as I had just found out that the woman clinging closely to the right of the provocative blonde was her girlfriend, and she was behaving like a dog guarding a bone. "Wait!" Emma stood right in front of me, staring into my eyes with an astonished kind of look about her. "How the fuck is it that no one here's interested in me? I'm not that repulsive! Or am I?" Even though she sounded really serious, I couldn't help laughing. "No one's interested in you because you're straight." Emma smirked and took a sip of her drink before continuing "what's that got to do with it? It's not written in capital letters on my forehead." A guy standing nearby, listening to our conversation, leaned over to kiss Emma on the cheek. "Darling, we sound each other out with the gay radar and you are way off our charts." I laughed as I watched my sister who was now dancing raunchily with her new friend, joined quickly by Alina.

Angelica is staring at me with an expression that is a combination of amusement and pity.

"You mean to tell me that in the exact moment that you found your balance and had the energy to build something you threw yourself into another relationship?" Before I could answer, she turned over two cards and banged her hand down on the table so hard that the tablecloth lifted, filling up with air, almost as if it too were sighing with disappointment at the choices I'd made in the past. "And not just a fling! You fell for her, hook, line and sinker!" She stops asking me questions and proceeds to rummage through my past with the Tarot cards, with surgical precision. Of course, standing with my hands shoved into my pockets, looking back at my life as if it were a film, it's very easy to judge, even for me, and I know all the whys and wherefores. For Angelica, who has no idea of the background details, it is even easier.

At least I think it is.

I remember being full of enthusiasm at the time, and I poured all of my energy into Alina, who was so different from all the others that I was convinced I had found "The One". Two months after we met, we were already living together and trying to merge our separate lives into one, with no difficulty whatsoever. We couldn't be apart even for a moment, but the signs of the previous relationship were still clearly visible, both to me and to her. We had to win each other's trust and so we founded our relationship on absolute transparency and the complete absence of surprise, and on boredom. At the end of the first year, we were already like an old couple, more in terms of our habits than our attitudes, because we spent four nights a week clubbing and had started working together. Alina, with her inflexible, reliable character, had given me what an unsuitable mother had never managed to give me. At last, I felt as though someone was taking care of me. I abided by the house rules and this concept of family life was the closest I'd ever come to what I'd caught glimpses of in the homes of my friends.

"That wasn't love girl! Your head and your heart were full. You needed it so much that, on the very first occasion that presented itself, you opened the floodgates of your feelings and convinced yourself." Angelica made me smile. She was as passionately involved in this reading as if it were a soap and she kept looking at me between one harsh judgment and the next as if she couldn't wait to see how it ended.

"Angelica don't you think that everyone falls in love because the time is right? When your heart is ready and you want to really live life to the full?"

The fortune teller regained her composure and, looking as though she was of a completely different opinion, lit another cigarette. "That's not love. Love is what pushes you to leave even when you don't want to, because you know that you're damaging yourself. Your return to Turin was an expression of love. Love is about living in order to move forward, it's not about involvement. You took shelter in a relationship because you were afraid of facing everything on your own. That way, if you had failed, you would have been able to find an excuse."

Was she playing dirty because she had already read the epilogue of my story with Alina on the table strewn with cards or had she just guessed?

Day by day, we kept building professional and personal castles which systematically collapsed. Alina was indomitable, with an iron-fisted rule, the result of her growing up in Russia, and a deceitful nature that she had developed during an eight-year relationship with a rather unsuccessful drug dealer. The only things he had succeeded in were getting himself arrested and leaving Alina crippled by debt and surrounded by a host of very shady acquaintances. She was prepared to do anything to make sure that our relationship and our working life proceeded, moving smoothly and naturally between what was legal and what was not.

My business partnership with Augusto who had, in the meantime, become one of Ada's best friends, had inspired me to open a studio of my own. This meant that I was completely free to choose who I wanted to work with and which artistic projects I wanted to pursue, and it seemed the most natural thing in the world to ask her to work with me.

Alina had an innate spirit of self-preservation which encouraged her to defend herself before her family, even though she wasn't aware of it. Consciously, she went to work and washed the dishes after dinner, and subconsciously she hid money at the bottom of a drawer, for emergencies. But just for "her" emergencies because, when the stash of cash eventually surfaced, there had been a whole series of emergencies that the "emergency fund" had completely ignored.

Consciously, she had no problem living with my little dog, but when Oscarina almost died after a sterilisation op gone wrong, she had no problem in leaving me at the vets on my own and coming back home to sleep. "There's no point in both of us staying. At least tomorrow I'll be rested so I can be there for you when you need me". Oscarina survived the night but my feelings for Alina gradually began to weaken.

As far as our sex life was concerned, we had found a peaceful harmony that was a bit like a nocturnal appointment with an old hairdresser who knows how you like your hair and does everything she can to make sure you leave the salon satisfied, with no surprises. Trimming our sexual split-ends had become an increasingly rare event. One evening, at dinner, I tried talking to her about the rut we'd fallen into and the lack of initiative. All I got in exchange was a 1930s textbook seduction scene, with a handkerchief draped over the bedside lamp, background music and Alina kissing my hand like she did when she was seducing the young girls in the clubs, who went wild for the lesbian bartender in the best gay venue in town. From that evening onwards, the split-ends of our relationship were left to deteriorate, and my attention inevitably started to wander. This didn't escape Alina's cold, watchful eyes. Being well-versed in the art of trying to make people feel guilty, while seeming absolutely blameless herself, she took up some of her old habits, which she knew I hated. The fact that she found herself in the bathroom of a club with an old friend, sniffing coke, was the result of my indifference. Going out to dinner with a crowd of her drug dealer pals was a way of getting back in touch with herself. Accusing me of not going to funeral of her ex-boyfriend's mother and then wondering whether she should marry him because, united by their pain, they had thought about reuniting as a couple, was quite normal according to her, while the fact that I was left speechless and then decided to leave were proof of my selfishness. Leaving wasn't actually possible because Alina's attitude made it quite clear that she would make me pay for humiliating her both financially and emotionally. She had access to my entire client book and regularly threatened to sell it to another studio that she had contacted during our arguments.

Our relationship had dwindled to nothing more than work and forced cohabitation and despite the fact that she did everything she could to pretend this wasn't the case, every time she went back to Russia to visit her family, I felt like I could finally breathe again, realising that I would be much better off without her.

One evening, I start chatting with a girl on Facebook, dusting off those old but subtly seductive attitudes that I found so much fun. I'd recently even begun thinking that perhaps Ada had been right after all and that there was nothing wrong with a bit of harmless flirting. The flirting went a little bit further every day until I craftily asked her to meet me at a party where I was going to be with Alina. The battle was over quickly but the wounds kept festering for weeks. A series of coincidences and copious amounts of vodka created one big disaster, leaving me with the same astonished expression that children have when they've broken a glass which, during its fall, has destroyed the glass table and the floor tiles. An unstoppable domino effect that I would never be able to erase from her mind. Not that it really bothered me. I believe that the universe sometimes works sadistically to put us where we're supposed to be and, if all this hadn't happened, the swamp of habit and resignation that we'd fallen into would probably have swallowed us up until we grew old.

Patrizia arrived after a calculated delay and, after all the sexting we'd been doing, the expectations were high. I don't what I thought I was going to achieve, bearing in mind that I was there with Alina and there was no real chance of being able to go off somewhere without her. Throughout the evening, while I waited for Patrizia to arrive and Alina bought drinks for everyone, we drank an indefinite number of cocktails. I think I must have convinced myself that I had developed the gift of invisibility, because I kept unashamedly exchanging glances with Patrizia and touching her. And she, of course, did the same. Typically Mediterranean, a tease with doe-like eyes, she was exactly my type of woman at that time, and more importantly, she was the complete opposite of Alina who, seated at the bar, weighed up all of our movements with her icy stare. After watching us brush hands for the umpteenth time, Alina dragged me outside and we launched into an argument which, fuelled by too much alcohol, ended theatrically with her telling me it was over between us and leaving with one of her drug dealer friends. I ended up stumbling towards the car, followed by some drunken guy who wanted to take me home. That was when it all kicked off. Too drunk to drive, I stopped in a factory carpark on the way home and slept there until morning. Far from sober, I somehow managed to make my way home and found Alina holding one of my phones (the one you use for things you don't want anyone to know about) and with the contents of my bag tipped out onto the table. She had found the texts and was even more furious than the night before. What happened next, though, was what triggered my fury. The receipt for a hotel room where I'd spent a few hours on my own, in one of those moments when I needed to get to grips with myself and make some decisions about my life, was in my bag. Living with Alina meant that I couldn't take time out for myself, so I'd invented a story about going to see Emma to discuss a family emergency. I had come home without having reached any decision, but much calmer, and had completely forgotten about the receipt. It was the truth but there was no way I was going to change Alina's mind because she'd now gotten to the point where she saw everything as proof of my carnal betrayal with someone I'd never done anything more than flirt with. I found the whole thing quite funny because, in actual fact, I had been unfaithful to Alina, but earlier on in our relationship, in a moment of madness with a mutual friend, but I hadn't said anything to avoid hurting her. Whether being unfaithful is right or wrong, it's still a betrayal, and washing your conscience clean by confessing, and hurting the other person, is an excellent way to move on, passing the buck to someone else. It was me who'd made the mistake and I had already decided to leave Alina as soon as she found a job, so being accused of betraying her with Patrizia was just Karma's way of putting me back on the right track. After several useless and tiring attempts at convincing her, I ended up calling Patrizia and inviting her to the incriminated hotel and committing the crime that Alina had already sentenced me for. At least now she had a reason to insult me.

Clearly lacking all Sapphic experience and visibly embarrassed by the standard moves, after a few hours we found ourselves exchanging awkward looks and quickly leaving the hotel. We kept seeing each other for a few weeks (because women like to persevere and hate wasting time or admitting that they are wrong) and then lost touch. I found out some time later that she'd gotten married and had a daughter and I was pleased with myself for having realised that she was "far too straight to be a lesbian". Everyone has a right to happiness, and you can't pretend to be what you aren't.

Alina and I split up the way an elderly couple would. Initially we planned it all out very civilly but were at each other's throats in next to no time. The result was that I ended up sleeping on my sister Emma's couch (again) and Alina stayed in our flat, which was in my name, without paying any rent for about a year. That debt was joined by her car payments, which we conveniently forgot about.

Emma took one look at me, the dog and my cases and said, without too much ceremony, "you know I love you, but you have to have to get the fuck out of here in hurry".

8

I was always a very quiet and overly sensitive child, not because I didn't have anything to say but because I've always liked to observe things. The way my parents, my grandparents and everyone else around me behaved always gave me a lot of food for thought. The same can't be said for my peers, who rarely had anything of any interest to talk about. I enjoyed spending my time with adults, or at least I thought I did, because they sated my hunger for knowledge of the human soul and were far more entertaining than the television.
I must have been about seven at the time and I was watching her having breakfast, standing in front of the window. She was holding a cup of milky coffee in one hand and using the other to dunk biscuits into it. Staring outside, her shoulders tense, I could tell from her position that my mother was looking into

my grandparents' garden, a little green dot in the middle of all the concrete yards on the block of houses where we lived. That garden was where I went to play every day, where I had learned to climb the only tree that was in it. Every year, all of us grandchildren picked that tree's peaches, which were then handed out to all the neighbours. On peach-picking days, the lady who used to shout at us for anything and everything put up with our presence on her garage roof, almost going so far as to smile indulgently. The only time we had permission to climb onto the garage roof was to pick peaches, as I found to my dismay when I did it one winter afternoon. I was soundly punished by both my grandmother and mother and got a good telling off from our neighbour too.

"If you fall, you'll hurt yourself!" My mother looked sincerely alarmed and seemed convinced that she was absolutely right. Didn't it occur to them for one minute that I might actually fall when I was picking peaches? Or did the fact that I was doing something useful eliminate the risk? I wisely avoided asking because I'd learned that, in my family, logical thought was open to manipulation when it was convenient and that every concept, and what was considered acceptable or unacceptable, could be turned upside down to suit the individual. Turning tables and making excuses were the favourite sports of everyone in my family. The fact that this was already clear to me at such a tender age made me wonder whether I really was related to them, or whether I had been swapped over at the maternity hospital. I think I secretly wanted this to be the case. Growing up, I coloured this thought in a variety of shades, sometimes hoping I'd been adopted and other times assuming I had been put there by aliens. When I realised just how twisted the stories I wove to avoid believing that I was related to them were, I had to admit that those stories were the very things that made me their rightful heir.

My mother had been having breakfast, in her dressing gown, in front of the narrow window for several weeks, but that morning there was something different about her. She usually looked out over the empty garden in silence but that morning I could tell by the fact that she was standing so absolutely still that something was going on. All of a sudden, she jumped, stifling a scream as the milky coffee splashed onto the floor in a vain attempt to follow the cup which she had set down, none too carefully, on the washing machine next to the window. I was sitting at the kitchen table so it took me just a few seconds to reach my mother, who automatically grabbed my shoulders and shoved me in front of her in a very unmotherly way. From that spot I could clearly see what was happening in my grandparent's garden and I could hear my mother's heart thudding wildly in her chest against my head. Her hands were digging like claws into my shoulders and even if I had wanted to escape her grip to turn away, it would have been impossible. Another argument, more screaming and all the neighbours looking out of their windows, some worried, some annoyed and others merely nosey. My grandmother's furious anger swelled progressively as she blatantly sought the support of her audience, which got bigger and bigger, attracted by her screaming at my granddad, who just stood there, his arms folded, leaning up against the doorway. His dark face revealed his pain and anger. His lack of visible reaction was the consequence of his embarrassment and shame at being made a spectacle of, but also the result of his pyromaniacal nature, which led him to fan the flames of his wife's folly with words whispered under his breath. Apparently silent and inanimate, he muttered razor sharp answers that only fuelled the rage of my grandmother, who was fiercely brandishing an enormous pair of garden shears, along with her desire to perform to the crowd even more. It was a battle of dexterity and vendetta. He, unarmed, nimbly and cleverly avoiding her lunges, knowing all too well that he needed to find shelter, and she, clumsily uncoordinated but driven by the desire for satisfaction, which would come only when she drew blood. My mother's hands gripped my shoulders tighter and tighter and I could see her completely white knuckles, contrasting with her long red fingernails. My granddad, avoiding one of my grandmother's last lunges, decided to step to the right but then, hesitating for a second, failed to escape her final attempt. She threw all her weight against his chest as he withdrew, backing up and disappearing into the doorway. This time, after a moment of ghostly silence, the whole neighbourhood, not just my mother, began shouting and whispering in worried tones. My grandmother moved away from the door, finally satisfied and visibly calmer, wiping the blades of the shears automatically on her apron to clean away the blood. Even in my memories as an adult, the fact that she did it so naturally has always made me shudder much more than the attack itself. My granddad then reappeared from the doorway with an evident wound and a growing bloodstain on his sweater.

I can't remember exactly what happened next, apart from the arrival of the police (as usual) and the shouts of my grandmother as she tried to justify her actions with her compelling but crazed and incomprehensible logic. It was just a surface wound and, at the time, there were none of today's television talk shows to blow family arguments way out of proportion, so that evening the whole family sat down at the table together regardless of the day's events. Grandparents, parents, aunts and uncles making sarcastic comments and jokes about what had happened. Even my mother was laughing, despite missing no opportunity, between one wisecrack and the next, to mention how much they'd embarrassed themselves in front of the neighbours. And then suddenly, as if the need to be the centre of attention weren't only genetically inherited but also a volatile and immediately contagious disease: "And you scared my daughter to death! I tried to stop her from seeing but she was so shocked I couldn't hold her back! Then she started crying and wouldn't stop!" The subsequent laughter had no effect on me whatsoever. My whole family, either individually or collectively, made a habit of playing with my sensitivity because they'd discovered that I would cry at the drop of a hat and that I could even cry to order. "Cry... Go on, cry... There you go, she's crying!" My tears would be followed by a loud educational slap from my mother "at least now you're crying for a reason."

So what might have seemed to be my mother scolding my grandmother was actually a comment to make me cry and everyone else laugh. And cry I did, but not because she'd succeeded in her intent. For the first time in my life, I cried out of anger and frustration. None of what she had said was true. I hadn't been shocked, I hadn't cried and she hadn't tried to stop me from seeing. On the contrary, she'd held me right in front of her. I was crying because I knew that, if I tried to contradict her, she'd make me out to be a liar in front of everyone and then slap me when we got home. As well as crying to order, I had a reputation for being a liar because, before I'd learned what a bad idea it was to candidly contest my mother's claims, she had succeeded in convincing everyone that I was a cry-baby and a fibber. The fact that they all said they loved me anyway was of little consolation.

My mother had a technique for controlling my sister and me and even though, at first glance, it didn't seem invasive, you could often feel the terror that reigned in our house. Anyone who knew her found it impossible to understand how difficult our relationship was because the image that she portrayed to others was very different from the one she reserved for the two of us.

The flaring of her nostrils was a sign that we had learned to interpret. The spirit of observation and an ability to translate the cyclic nature of attitudes and consequences was a perfect training ground for me, giving me a notable advantage when it comes to interpreting the behaviour of the vast majority of people I've met in my life.

If her nostrils flared while she slowly closed her eyes, lifted a hand to her forehead and drew back her lips, we knew that we had to stop whatever it was we were doing immediately, because it meant she was really annoyed and the consequences would be exasperated depending on how much anger and frustration, accumulated for other reasons, she had to get rid of. If the nostrils moved during a discussion in public, we had to interpret the situation on the basis of the circumstances. Roughly speaking, it wasn't a good sign. Wrong answer: you'll get a slap when we get home. You accepted a sweet and shouldn't have because the right nostril said not to, even though my voice was inviting you to take it: you'll get a slap when we get home. You didn't notice the flaring nostrils and kept on playing instead of standing stock still, as if your batteries had run out: you'll get a slap when we get home.

And she never forgot! She might not have slapped you immediately. You could reach dinner time without a problem and you'd be relaxing and laughing at something on television and then, right out of the blue, while you were still smiling, the slap would hit you like a bucket of water. It would take your breath away and kill your happy expression, changing it to surprise and then tears. Human conditioning by linking a feeling of pain to a moment of relaxation and play. I switched from laughing to crying so often that, for a long time, every time one or the other thing happened, the opposite happened automatically, creating a lot of embarrassment and often making my schoolmates laugh hysterically and make fun of me.

Over the years, I've learned to hold back both laughter and tears and to express both pain and joy with the same composure.

...

Her bedroom door was locked.

Again.

The beep of the incoming text on my phone and on my sister's phone in her room wasn't long coming.

"Look after your sister. I'm tired and depressed. The pain is too bad and it isn't right for me to make you live like this. Don't try to save me, there's no point." The first few times were a succession of agitation, fear, terror, phone calls, ambulances and the police. After the fourth, all we felt was bored, annoyed and indifferent. We learned, at our own expense, that if someone really wants to commit suicide, they don't shout wolf time and time again, they just do it. So Emma poked her head out of her room without fully opening the door. "Did you get it too? I'm going out, are you staying in?" "No, I'm going out too, I have to work tonight".

We both just shrugged our shoulders and sent a text. "We're going out. You've got the house to yourself so you don't need to stay locked in your room. Don't leave the windows open because the cat will get out."

My mother cyclically announced that she was going on a "life strike", sometimes accompanied by fake suicide attempts, sometime refusing to eat (or just eating milk and biscuits where no one could see her) and, more often, admitting herself to a clinic for three months, during which I filled in for her at work so she wouldn't lose her job. The clinics she went to brought her immediately back to life, convincing her even more that my sister Emma and I were the cause of all her troubles. Things carried on like this for years, until the law changed, and you could only go to a clinic if you didn't treat it like a hotel. You could only leave the premises in the company of a relative, you couldn't have a phone or a computer and, above all, you had to really prove that you wanted to get better instead of just wallowing in self-pity. From that moment on, my mother said that clinics and the doctors who worked in them were all useless and began wading through the red tape necessary to have herself declared too depressed to go back to work. She succeeded. And as she got ready, every Friday evening, to go out dancing, looking as though she was being forced to go, my sister and I wondered how she was ever going to survive once she realised that she was completely alone, with no one on her side. She really didn't care. In the end, we had to accept the fact that we had been generated by a woman incapable of loving anyone but herself, who was happier without us. This said, our presence was of some use to her too, because of the maintenance our dad paid her, the family allowance cheque when she was working, and saving face with the rest of the family, in front of whom she declared that life without us wouldn't be worth living. We were never sure of one thing: did she do it deviously, on purpose? Or did the burden of being unable to feel sincere love for her daughters make her feel so awful that she regularly attempted to destroy herself?

9

It was a typical evening.

The club was the one where we'd first met. Alina had started working there again not long after we'd split up. We had established a sort of cold friendship which ignored the fact that she was living in my flat without paying any rent and that she was still telling our friends that I had cheated on her with Patrizia, and a whole load of other things that had gradually take on the guise of urban legends rather than things that had really happened. And me? Why had I decided to get ready to go out in heels to stand on the other side of the bar like a perfect best friend after that famous and interesting bartender had said such awful things to me and, about me, to our friends? Perhaps because, when a relationship comes to an end, your feelings change and transform, but they're still feelings. We had had some great times together and I thought it was best to think about the good ones and try to forget the bad, not for her benefit, for mine. So that I could grow and tackle my future relationships with a lot less anxiety. I didn't want to teach my heart to believe that every relationship hides that inevitable moment when the person you've shared part of your life with is destined to disappear forever. This is often what stops you from making decisions. You realise that your other half isn't a perfect fit but you don't want to lose them. Evolving physically was important in order for the survival of the species, evolving emotionally will perhaps bring mankind to believe in and protect humanity. I also missed that funny mishmash of characters, always the same crowd, who park themselves in Turin's historic gay club. Just like me. Last, but not least, I had convinced myself that I was part of the furniture. Leo saw me through the eyes of a partner in tragic crime and kept saying that we could call ourselves two victims of the now super popular Alina who, since we'd split up, had seduced and conquered hordes of young girls. Ex-boyfriend, ex-jailbird, ex-hetero, ex-builder, Leo was a good-natured jester who was capable of the most dreadful things. Fortunately, he also knew how to earn your forgiveness with his joie de vivre and clowning around. That evening, he had decided to tell me all about his life with Alina and, to conceal my boredom and awkwardness, I started looking around to see if I could see anyone new and worthy of interest. A mass of black hair and a nice arse sheathed in a pair of shiny latex trousers grabbed my attention. I unleashed the lorry driver that lives deep down inside me and, nudging Leo said: "what do you think of the brunette then?" Silence followed by laughter forced me to look him in the face and he made it immediately clear that there was no point in even thinking about it. Then, suddenly, my brain joined the dots.

"It's Alessandra, the Dominatrix, isn't it?"

The question was rhetorical and didn't require an answer. Shit!

The initial weak attraction immediately turned into resentment. This was the girl who had "cured" Alina of mourning for me.

It's pointless pretending it isn't true. Every time we leave someone, the longer their desperation lasts the more satisfied we secretly feel. That young girl had put an end to my ex's unhappiness, so it was only right and proper for me to dislike her. Huge pictures of her were scattered all over what was still my flat and the funniest thing of all was that the intriguing brunette with a passion for S&M wasn't in the least bit attracted to Alina, she simply enjoyed being courted and Alina did nothing but moan about it. Not that it mattered to me but there was something about the situation which sent shivers down my spine.

Then Alina noticed her and decided to introduce us. "This is Alessandra, and this is my ex". Fantastic! What a great introduction. I no longer deserved mention by name, only by category!

Alessandra sort of shook my hand, depositing her droopy appendage into mine, without even looking at me, turning around to talk to another piece of furniture instead. The problem is that mine has always been an excellent handshake and the minute she realised, she turned back to face me and looked me straight in the eye.

Halfway between surprised and astounded, her gaze came to rest on me, and the visual stimulus must have reached her brain too, because from that moment on, she decided not to take her eyes off me. And her two slaves followed her lead.

Whichever way I turned, Alessandra's two human hangers-on were staring at me, ready to report back to the Queen seated at the table who, glass in hand, was staring at a specific spot in the venue, lost in thought, her neck elegantly inclined to one side with her silky, smooth hair shining in the evening light. Her bare shoulders and muscular legs crossed to show off the red sole of her shoes. "Are you staring at her because you want to kill her or because you want to take her to bed?" Leo was always very elegant. I turned towards him, laughing, and as I did so, I realised that Alessandra wasn't the only one sending out her slaves to gather information on me. Alina was standing behind the bar pretending to talk to someone but, having lived with her for four years, I could easily spot the fact that her attention was focused on what she could see out of the corner of her eye and not what was going on straight ahead of her. So I made a show out of laughing loudly and shrugging as if to say, "I don't know". It was fun and there was no harm in enjoying the situation.

I had absolutely no intention of taking the Queen of Hearts and her two pages home with me!

The dancing was about to begin on the floor below and all the staff, including Alina, started heading downstairs to get everything ready.

As she'd done so many times before when we were together, she took the ice bucket and invited both Alessandra and her slaves, with a movement of her head, to follow her, giving me a filthy look as she disappeared with them downstairs. Smiling, I headed towards the bathroom to check my make-up and get ready for the evening.

"Hand-kissing".

One of the standard tactics of the Russian conqueror. I found her doing just that as I took off my coat, which was whisked away from me in exchange for a blue ticket with a number on it before I could change my mind.

"What do you want to drink?"

Still holding the rookie's hand just a couple of inches from her lips, Alina flashed a satisfied look disguised as sincere interest in what I wanted to order.

"Vodka and ice" I said, smiling casually. A deafening squeal almost made me drop my glass as I whipped around to see the source of the sudden acoustic pollution: it was the giggle of the young "dominatrix" who was talking loudly, in an incredibly squeaky and irritating voice, to Alina who turned around occasionally to smile at me. Convinced that she had Alessandra's undivided attention, she was devoting all her energy to showing off her conquest, without realising that Alessandra's interest was focused on the end of the bar, where I was sitting. Her two slaves were perfectly well aware of what was going on and never took their eyes off us for a moment. I was almost certain that they didn't even blink, but maybe I was letting my imagination run away with me. All of a sudden two hands came from behind my head to gently cover my eyes, while a hot kiss on my neck made me forget for a second that I was in a public place. My smile must have been really dazzling because when I moved the hands away from my face, both Alina and Alessandra had a furious glimmer in their eyes.

Elena. One of those people you can't help but be attracted to. Beautiful, clever, just the right amount of bitchiness and incredibly entertaining, she was another one of those women that Alina thought I'd been unfaithful to her with, one of the urban legends that had done the rounds. We had spoken to each other a few weeks earlier and had joked about the possibility of giving everyone something real to talk about. Obviously, she had decided it was time to put the plan into practice. Nothing had ever happened between me and Elena, apart from a kiss before I met Alina. Our relationship was characterised by explicit conversations and games which could apparently be misconstrued as sexual. In actual fact, we had so much fun that the thought of having to justify them, especially now that we were both single, didn't even cross our minds.

She greeted everyone in the club, including Alina, with her usual energy and ordered a drink, with one for me too. She was like a loud fairground entertainer and I loved her for it. Sensual and seductive, as you got to know her better you realised that she was a wayward little girl who wanted to play because her adult life was really hard work and far too complicated. She would show up out of the blue and then disappear again just as quickly, for days, months or even years. The beauty of our relationship was that time never changed anything. Wrapped up in telling each other the latest news, I forgot about the game with Alina, Alessandra and her subjects, but their glances didn't escape Elena who, with a conspiratorial smile, rubbed her hands together and took me to dance in the middle of the floor. Not even a minute had gone by and she was dancing with two men and a girl wearing a very masculine jacket and tie. Elena couldn't resist her; she likes her women rough and masculine. I was about to go back to the table when I found myself with Alessandra's face just half an inch from mine. Her eyes were glued to mine but there was no kind of physical contact, other than the gentle touch of her breath against my cheek. She looked like she was going to kiss me but the imperceptible movements of her body as she danced shifted the tiny space between us without ever giving us the chance to touch each other. There was something intriguing about the deliberate sensuality of the little dominatrix. I decided to go along with her game, elegantly avoiding looking at Alina. I wanted to enjoy the moment without christening it with any kind of spitefulness or vengeance. The girl was pure fire and she spread her flames with just a few, essential gestures. Astounded, I asked myself whether the vodka was playing its part in the chemistry between us but continued playing the game while the two unnerving presences at Alessandra's service kept on bringing her drinks before backing away one curtsey after the other. Evidently the little princess was convinced that she'd seduced and convulsed me because when I dropped a soft kiss on her lips and went back to sit down next to Elena, she stood motionless and raging for a fraction of a second before turning away and continuing to dance.

"God, she's interesting! I just find it strange imagining the two of you fucking in front of a couple of spectators who do a Mexican wave every time she climaxes". Elena's expression was so serious and thoughtful, as she drank her glass of wine, that we burst out laughing like two schoolgirls, infuriating the person that neither of us was paying any attention to at all.

"You two are always scheming together! Instead of pissing my garden why don't you go and do it somewhere else?" Alina had planted herself in front of our table and was looking at us as if she was waiting for an answer. I picked up my empty glass and placed it on Alina's tray, smiling: "you always tend to become bitter at this time of night. We weren't laughing at you if that's what's bothering you". Elena emptied her glass and put it down next to mine. "We'll have another two. We need to refill our munitions to piss in your garden!" Saying goodbye to all remaining elegance, Alina gave us the finger and went back to the bar.

"She's just hysterical because she's realised that Cleopatra and her slaves can't take their eyes off you." It was true and I had to admit that all that attention was starting to have an effect. Elena had noticed and started imagining us dating, with the most unlikely and unpredictable situations, due to Alessandra's job.

The evening could have ended with a slice of pizza sitting next to the river if Elena's conquest hadn't decided to invite her elsewhere. She didn't wait to be asked twice and disappeared at the speed of light, leaving me with the two drinks that had just been brought to the table and filled with the desire to leave just as quickly with the girl who continued to stare at me. The desire was obviously mutual because, with calculated slowness, Alessandra began walking towards me with a hint of a satisfied smile on her face.

At the start of the evening, I'd been annoyed by that mysterious looking frivolous girl and any attitude I'd had would have been mistaken for suffering or nostalgia for Alina, despite the fact that I wasn't actually jealous, only disappointed. In women, pride can become the beginning of madness unless it's accompanied by awareness and I could quite easily have mistaken that annoyance and that desire to cause trouble for a signal that led me back to Alina.

Fortunately, I realised that it was blind territoriality and, as if by magic, the bitterness towards the Dominatrix faded, giving way to curiosity mixed with dislike which, as she drew closer, gradually turned into something else.

10

74

There were no such things as points of view with her because she changed her mind and her vision of the world every fifteen minutes. One day she wanted to breed horses and the day after she wanted to design glamour T-shirts and sell them online. She dreamed of opening a sort of farm to grow organic produce but loved the idea of moving to New York.

It was like living with a ten-year-old child who still hadn't progressed beyond the phase of constantly asking "why" but had incorporated every international porn star into the way she behaved.

Initially, this dichotomy had trapped me into having no idea how much she pretended to be an airhead and how much she really was.

She really was. An airhead I mean.

And, just like a ten-year-old child, she succeeded in winning me over with her naivety, irritating me with her lies, annoying me with her moods and spoiling our relationship with her tantrums.

When I got to know her, I noticed that her personality had a certain undefined similarity with that of Ada and, for a long time, I believed that they were similar, but I wasn't sure why. Then I realised that what made them similar in my eyes stemmed from the selfishness, the tantrums and the fact that neither of them loved me, just the idea of security and reliability that I mysteriously inspire in people.

The fact that I had fallen in love with a young girl who had decided to make a living out of being a Dominatrix, and had two unbearably slimy slaves who drooled over her on a daily basis, should have made me think about myself and not her.

 At this point, Angelica laughs in a way that doesn't quite fit with the mysterious and aristocratic air she's trying to convey to me and the passers-by. Between one question and another, we are taking a rather embarrassing stroll through my past. It's as if wanting to see only the downside of what has happened to us in the past is a way of making ourselves better in the present. But what we are today isn't only the result of our choices; it's also the result of what we felt when we made them. It isn't as if, every time we decide something, we concentrate on a cosmic connection with farsightedness. I personally jump into things and then realise what I've done later. Maybe this is why the reading of my past seems so exhilarating.

"Did no one ever tell you that it's fine to be alone without jumping from one bed to another? What are you – the gay version of the Fonz?" And she continues laughing in my face. Shameless and satisfied. She shakes her head and points to the pack of cards again. I cut it to the right and wait.

Some people come into your life and you notice their beneficial effects immediately. Others disguise themselves in joyful mystery and drag you into a turbine of emotions that gradually make you different, making tiny yet important changes to your character and the way you behave. You almost convince yourself that all this is for the best because often the direct synonym of the word change is the word positive. From the very first moment, Alessandra had drawn me into a spiral of urgent and primitive desire.

Everything was dictated by the physical need for contact with her skin and her lips. Yet every time I paused to listen to what she was saying, I realised that I was reasoning with my vagina and, being unable to accept the fact that I was so superficial, I decided to end the relationship every day.

But just like an ex-smoker or an ex-alcoholic, the first drag or the first sip was enough to devastate my good intentions.

The fact that she was so different from everything I had ever known before while being so similar to what I had wanted to experience in the past bewitched me. To be honest, nothing about her was actually alluring in its own right.

She was a Dominatrix.

She made a living out of letting people lick her feet. She would meet strangers in hotel rooms and make them strip naked before allowing them to ejaculate on her toes.

Fetishists, submissives, slaves and masochists. The BDSM world can be very serious and complex, as I found out when I started studying and frequenting it, but not in the way that Alessandra did. Submissive without even realising it, she was happy with her life as a fake queen in a fake castle made up of lingerie and sex toys. One of her favourites used to reduce her to the limits of exhaustion with cheap beer and joints.

She has never been a particularly brilliant person. It always took her quite a while to work things out. Not because she was stupid, just because was incredibly disorganised. Her conversations were made up of unlikely mental images and incomprehensible monologues which jumped from pillar to post. To keep up with her, you had to be completely out of your head or have a clear intention to manipulate her.

There was nothing to it really. Her incredible naivety made her the perfect subject for filling her head with ideas and making sure that, the following day, she would proudly pass them off as her own. This side of her was blatantly obvious and, being in love with her, I started watching everyone with suspicion, without ever imagining that my suspicions should also have been directed at her.

"When they make alcohol-free beer how do they remove the alcohol from the bottles?" It was three o'clock in the morning and, after an unspecific number of joints, bottles of wine and beer, she had come out with this question. I laughed so much because the idea of little gnomes having to eliminate alcohol from bottles of beer seemed really comical. I thought she was laughing with me, but her questions were deadly serious. They repeatedly created moments of absolute hilarity over the years but, more often not, they were embarrassing. Stuck in the rush-hour traffic in Turin, all I could think about was that, at the end of the day, I would see Alessandra and we would have a fabulous time, but I also knew that I would end up neglecting the dogs and my work again, and this was starting to bother me. Her constant avoidance of talking about her job had become the cause of regular arguments, and consuming copious amounts of alcohol was the only way for us to let go and relax. At the umpteenth red light with the umpteenth rose-seller, my phone rang. Her slightly subdued voice feigned a casual tone: "I love you. I'll see you tonight. I can't wait."

I asked her if she was in the bathroom making herself beautiful for me and was struck by her hesitation, followed by a giggle. And then we said goodbye. After four traffic lights, two windscreen-washers and five thousand mountains made out of molehills, in which I tried to convince myself I was just being paranoid, the phone rang again. "I'm sorry, I lied to you, I'm at Dani's". She'd lied to me again. A session normally lasts an hour. It was gone midnight when she finally got home, drunk, stoned and filled with intentions of spending the whole night mimicking D-series porn films, with requests for sips of wine and glasses of water during the intervals.

At that time, my version of love was a clear expression of masochism which I just couldn't break away from. A shameful habit that I couldn't explain to my friends or even to myself. Maybe I needed to hurt myself for having made such a huge mistake in letting myself go with someone who was so wrong for me.

But I was too proud and stubborn to admit that I'd gotten it all wrong so I tried to put things right without realising that all I was doing was destroy myself even more.

It was like trying to train an incontinent dog not to wee all over the place. Every time I thought I was getting somewhere I'd find a new stain on the carpet.

I was frustrated. I often got the impression that I was in a relationship with a dark-haired caricature of Paris Hilton, but with no money, no hotels and no reason whatsoever to have such a high opinion of herself. Our first sexual encounter made everything clear. Typical occasional sex with someone you like but with whom there isn't really a spark. The week after our first meeting at the club where Alina worked, we met again in another club on the other side of town. There was no doubt that we intended to seduce each other, and the result was instantaneous. We'd tasted each other's lips for the first time during that meeting and liked it so much that we dumped the slaves and escaped to my house. Limbs entwined and gasping for breath, one trying to predict the other's movements in order to find a rhythm that would satisfy both of us. Requests disguised as moaning denials and the impression that it was more of an athletic performance than anything else. Despite the embarrassment of the first time, the passion was palpable perhaps because it was so different. It was purely the physical act that guided our instincts and kept us united in the thought that we had been right in getting together. Such an intense involvement could only be the demonstration of a union that was meant to be. After the first orgasm, the embrace became typically feminine and emotional. That joining of bodies that is the prelude to the exclusive relationship, to jealousy and to the desire to do it again, immediately and forever. Physical love between two women isn't plagued by the fact that they might not climax, but with Alessandra I realised that it can be challenging anyway. Especially for her, as I was to find out later.

I've never had to work so hard to satisfy a woman. Not that hard work bothers me. It was the fact that she was always so detached that turned me off completely, to the point where it became just a mechanical action, aggravated by the sense of competition and her habit of using extra powerful vibrators. I felt like I was a stick blender with a high-speed mode complex. The fact that she was a dominatrix often overflowed into the sex between us. She would sort of drift off and then suddenly explode into a series of moans that seemed false and reminded me of an orgasm straight off youPorn. All that was missing to make it complete was some buffering and adverts. But she wasn't faking, it was her detached way of seeing sex that made her so introspective throughout before exploding at the end. This astonished me and left me feeling as though I had no role at all to play, at least not until she clung onto me with all her strength when she came. This had excited me in the beginning but then I had tried to vary things a bit. We even went to a psychologist who explained that people who masturbate a lot are very selfish during sex with others and apparently everything works one-way but this is only an impression created by the type of mental and emotional concentration triggered in relation to pleasure.

When she decided to play an active role, things got even worse. Lots of girls are convinced that, to make a woman come they have to push so hard and so deep as to almost tickle her tonsils. Did they all have ambitions of becoming explorers when they grew up? The monotony and pointlessness of this endless hammering away was compounded by the fact that, instead of looking lustfully and passionately into my eyes, she would stare at her own tattooed arm, fascinated by the swelling of her biceps.

It isn't surprising that enormous amounts of alcohol accompanied our evenings, and this improved our sexual chemistry, as often happens when you bring a third party into a couple. We added a series of sex toys and vibrators into our routine, spicing everything up with some healthy role playing too.

Later, when I was able to think more clearly, I wondered why I'd never put a stop to the situation, which was damaging for both of us. Where does my need to look after someone begin and where does my self-destruction and arrogance end? Was it that I just couldn't admit that I'd been wrong? How was it possible that the incredible physical attraction confused me so much, especially when the sex really wasn't that incredible at all? Could it be that my mother's madness hadn't skipped a generation but had simply affected me differently? Does heterosexual madness change when you pass on your genes to a homosexual? Or is loneliness so terrifying that even the wrong relationship is better than no relationship at all? One evening, she came home, her eyes bloodshot with anger, and planted herself in front of me, ready for battle. She was beautiful, her silky-smooth hair was hanging loose, framing her face, her eyes were shining and her lips were just slightly parted. Her light dress was moulded to her whole body.

"What's this supposed to mean?" And she threw the telephone on the couch. She was actually very nice about it because, despite the rage, she avoided throwing it directly in my face.

"What am I supposed to say? I don't have to tell you anything! You lost the right to explanations from me when you refused to get rid of your slimy slaves!"

She opened her arms and stamped her foot on the floor.

"I've stopped being a dominatrix! I don't charge them anymore; I'm just trying to build a different kind of relationship with them. We've been friends for ages. And I've done all this for you because you helped me realised that it's better for me."

It was true, this was exactly what she thought. She was sincerely convinced that she'd made some significant changes. "Friends? Since when do friends pay to see each other? Or give each other sexy underwear?"

She kneeled down in front of me to look me straight in the eye. "But I can't control what they do, I'm not allowed to give them orders; isn't that what you wanted?" She had a satisfied smile on her face, thinking she'd forced me into a corner.

But she hadn't reckoned with my anger. "Does this make it alright for you to go and sunbathe on that arsehole's terrace and wear the underwear he gives you while you let him serve you ice-cold beer and slaver all over you?"

And then all of a sudden it dawned on her. She'd finally grasped the meaning of the text I'd sent her, which had triggered the rage and the telephone-throwing display.

"Alina told you! She promised me she wouldn't."

"And you still trust her? Look at yourself! You say you love me and then try to hide the things you do with the help of my ex-girlfriend, who also just happens to be someone you used to screw around with, and who can't wait to get back into her rightful place, wherever that is."

Alessandra was pacing up and down the living room, rubbing the back of her neck.

"I really don't know what it is you want from me."

She had said it sincerely, convinced that all her actions were justifiable in the name of the changes she was making.

But if you marry someone who's unfaithful to you and then promises they won't do it again, only to make the occasional slip-up, it's not like you can just forgive them.

"For fuck's sake! It's not like getting sober!" I wanted to end the relationship there. I didn't want to see her anymore but, at the same time, I wanted to rip her clothes off and stop wasting time talking.

And she knew.

"You know as well as I do that we should stop arguing and find a more creative way to decide the winner of this match". She slipped out of her dress as she spoke and walked towards me in the bloody underwear that had caused the argument in the first place. It was like a cold shower, simultaneously putting out my desire and reigniting my rage. "That's how you solve everything isn't it? But I've got no cash on me. Do you take credit cards?"

"You aren't calling me a whore, are you?" Her voice became a furious high-pitched shriek as she pulled on her dress and shoes.

"No, I'm not calling you a whore. You're just an idiot who's such a victim of male supremacy that you're convinced that charging someone for pretending to dominate them and making them come is a way to enhance your femininity. You aren't honest enough to be a whore."

Alessandra was so livid that she started to shake. And I just couldn't hold back. "But if I were to give you a present now, everything would probably go back to normal, wouldn't it?"

She walked away and shut herself in the bathroom, where she waited, crying and in vain, for me to go and apologise. I must have fallen asleep because I have a vague memory of a door slamming and of a piece of paper with a lipstick kiss on it and the word "goodbye", followed by a heart.

I'd like to be able to say that I never saw her again but the fact that I didn't run after her and didn't call her had exactly the opposite effect. She came back, threw herself at my feet and begged me to forgive her, saying she would really change. We both knew she wouldn't, but our relationship continued, with some substantial differences which required a fair amount of effort by both of us.

Once we'd smoothed out the rough spots that annoyed us about each other, our paths began to divide emotionally and, for a long time, all that was left was sex.

We became very close friends who occasionally relaxed together. We'd go on holiday, out for the day or to dinner and, at last, there was no more tension. The anxiety of making everything perfect had gone, because you can't ruin a relationship when you've already decided it's never going to work.

11

Alina had invited me to that exhibition to introduce me to Erica, the woman she had finally found peace with and with whom she had fallen in love after a series of adventures that she'd thrown herself into after coming to terms, with no shortage of difficulty, with my relationship with Alessandra.

Erica was really likeable, which was just as well because her physical appearance didn't do justice to her sunny nature and spirit of adventure. A dynamic and brilliant woman stuck in a body used as the television standard for the "ugly girl". Alina had mentioned it to me over the phone but hadn't been descriptive enough and then our conversation had turned to something else. "She makes me feel good, but there's something that makes me think it won't last." Her voice on the phone was flat and distracted as if she was doing something else.

"OK, well you just concentrate on the fact that she makes you feel good for now! You don't have to get married tomorrow!"

"Yes, but she's ugly!"

"Excuse me! What did you say?"

"Erica. She isn't what you'd call attractive. She isn't actually normal come to think of it"

"It sounds like you're describing a mutant" I laughed and so did Alina.

"Don't be stupid. You know what I mean!"

"But if you like her, I can't see the problem"

"The problem is that I'm happy, but I can't help noticing her appearance, and then I feel ashamed."

"What's there to feel ashamed about? If she doesn't have a pretty face and you notice it, that doesn't make you a bad person."

"No, I feel ashamed of the fact that my friends are going to see me with her." "Ah, that makes things different then. That does make you a bad person".

Alina laughed, thinking I was joking.

"At least people see you around town with someone like Alessandra! With a girlfriend that gorgeous what do you have to be ashamed of?"

"Nothing, but there are things about Alessandra's life that a lot of people might not like. I'm just bothered about the fact that she makes ME happy."

"Of course you're happy! I'd be happy to concentrate on that arse too!" "Ali, you make so many comments about arses that sometimes I get the feeling you're turning into a man."

Still laughing, she asked: "will you be bringing Ale or are you quite happy to keep on screwing her without taking her out?" "We do go out, it's just that we don't go clubbing. You know she's vilely jealous. Anyway, she can't come because it's her grandma's birthday." She said goodbye in a tone of voice that was somewhere between relieved and disappointed.

You couldn't tell how long Erica's hair was because it resembled a curlew's nest. The colour was halfway between light brown and burnt blonde with dark roots that needed some attention. Small but not slim, her eyes were too close together and a pair of glasses with jam jar-bottom lenses made them look very small. Her lips were very thin, and she had a moustache which bleaching had made even more noticeable.

She had a decidedly masculine appearance which extended to both her choice of clothes and the way she behaved. She'd open doors to let both Alina and me through, and always paid the bill, wherever we were.

I looked at Alina and wondered what she saw in this strange girl full of nervous tics.

"After the exhibition we could go and get a line".

So that was it! That was what had brought the two young ladies together.

"I don't smoke coke." And she didn't have nervous tics.

Erica smiled as if she didn't believe me. "You don't have to smoke it; you can sniff it. We can just hang out." Alina looked at me without making a sound, as if I'd uncovered an embarrassing secret.

"Thanks Erica, but I have to go home to my dogs and I'm seeing Alessandra tonight."

"Call me Ica. Maybe next time then."

She turned around and focused all her attention on her phone. The day had been fun, apart from the suggestion that we go and do drugs together.

Angelica was looking at me as if I were a painting by Salvador Dalí, tilting her head to one side and then the other, trying to read the expression on my face.

"Seriously! I've met lots of people who get carried away by things, but you deserve a prize."

"So you think that following your instinct is wrong?"

Angelica looks more and more like a sort of oracle before which I have the opportunity to analyse myself out loud, sounding a little less crazy than I would if I were to do it on my own.

"It's not throwing yourself into situations that's wrong. But staying in them at all costs, the way you do, is." She stares at me and then very slowly touches my forehead with her index finger. "There's no point in trusting your heart when you make decisions if you're going to let your brain guide you when it comes to putting them into practice."

"It all depends on me in both cases, it doesn't make any difference." Angelica smiles and shakes her head "what a load of crap. Not even you believe that and you're the one who said it." She takes three cards from the pack and then two more.

"How long were you with Ada?"

"Four years"

"Why did it last so long?"

"Because I was in love with her"

Angelica leans closer to my face again to gaze more intensely into my eyes "but you knew she wasn't the woman for you at the end of your first year together, the cards don't lie and nor does your memory".

I move, in an attempt to avoid her gaze and, fully aware of what she's getting at, I challenge her: "you aren't telling me anything I don't already know. I spent the next three years trying to make things work, trying to change Ada, to smooth out both myself and our life."

"Exactly. You wasted time"

"no, because, in the meantime, I lived and loved"

"but not to the full! You hid behind an act so you wouldn't have to throw yourself into the unknown. You've been a pathetic excuse for a woman who's always needed romance to move forward and, what's worse is that you didn't do it out of fear but out of selfishness, and you just did the same thing over and over again!"

"Ok, fine, calm down!"

We stare at each other for a few seconds and then burst into noisy laughter. The curious passers-by take Angelica's business card and, still laughing, she starts shuffling the tarot cards again. "You're good for business, I'll have to let you ask a few more questions for free!"

"Angelica, may I remind you that I've not asked any questions at all and, more importantly, you haven't given me any answers".

"This is actually turning out to be a very interesting reading. I'd better cancel the next appointment so we can dig deeper."

12

Emma's bar was full of people.

I'd been amazed when she decided to open it, considering my sister's solitary nature and especially her manifest hatred of people in general. She was comfortably seated at a table with a book and a glass of rum while the waitresses ran back and forth with full trays.

"Are you on strike?"

Emma looked up with a bored expression, clearly not happy with the idea of having to talk.

"No, I'm reading. What do you want?"

"It's nice to see you too"

She shut the book and picked up the glass, gesturing to tell me to look towards the far end of the room.

"Considering the meeting, I thought I'd best grab a front row seat."

Alina, Alessandra, Erica and three other girls whose names I didn't know were sitting at a table and seemed to be waiting for something.

"Just in case you haven't recognised the only three you haven't moved in with a minute after meeting them, let me help you out so then you can go and get ripped to shreds." Emma nodded at Linda, one of the waitresses, who brought over another glass of rum.

"You'll need it." And she handed me the glass to toast to what looked like a situation I was going to come out of with a few bruises.

"One's called Roberta, the one with the curly hair. That's the girl you had on karaoke night here. The one with the tattoo on her neck is Veronica, the insurance agent you mysteriously disappeared with after inviting her to see your studio, and the last one, the one with her elbows on the table, is Viviana, the girl who delivers the bread every morning and who you thought it would be a good idea to get to know more intimately last week."

I was dumbstruck. "You're not getting laid enough if you spend your time recording my dates in chronological order."

"No, it's you that's causing trouble in my bar." We were both laughing and Linda seemed amused by the situation too.

Emma got up to start working again "I have to go and sort things out for the aperitifs. Try not to detonate a lesbian bomb because I have a place full of people".

I approached that table of delights, with Alina's gaze focused on me and with Ica laughing shamelessly.

"Hello girls! What an interesting table." I bent over to give Alessandra a long, sensual kiss. I had greeted her the way you greet your woman, excluding everyone else at the table. As though there was no one else there, I whispered in her ear: "I've missed you" and then I sat down next to her.

If you kiss and tame the most beautiful member of a group of angry women, the female competitive instinct will prevail over the anger, which will be channelled directly to the need to be the centre of attention. Or at least that's what I was hoping would happen.

"Ica and I brought Alessandra here so that Roberta, Veronica and Viviana could meet her since you didn't think it was necessary to introduce them."

"While you, Alina, feel the need to mediate the situation by virtue of what exactly?"

I took Alessandra's hand in mine and she kept her head down as the tears welled up in her eyes. She had really made some changes to her life recently. She had abandoned the slaves forever and enrolled in evening classes to get a diploma, and she had made some real friends. Of course this hadn't done much to change our situation because it had come too late, but I was sincerely fond of her. She only thought she was madly in love with me because she still didn't have the strength to move forward alone in her new life.

"You know we all know each other." Alina was enjoying herself.

"Don't you mean that I've stumbled back into your huge garden again?"

Alessandra lifted her head up with a half-smile, having regained her confidence.

"Come on, girls. Since we're all here, why don't we have a drink and then go out and have some fun together? I don't want to ruin the night by listening to gossip."

Veronica smiled and stood up as if she couldn't wait to do just that, and the other two followed suit "we were just thinking the same thing. Alina insisted we meet for a drink but we had no idea we were going to find ourselves in this situation."

Roberta kissed my cheek, followed by the other two girls, and walked quickly out of the restaurant.

Ica started clapping but Alina's expression killed the applause immediately.

"Alina, even if it had been true, that wasn't the way to do it. It wasn't elegant at all." Alessandra had spoken calmly and without resentment.

"Ale, if it is true and you're being taken the piss out of, would that be elegant?"

Alessandra squeezed my hand tighter. "Well that would be my problem, not yours."

Erica and Alina left without saying goodbye and Alessandra turned to look at me. I had remained absolutely silent, watching this girl who never stopped amazing me.

"Now do you want to tell me why you go whoring about around town?"

"I don't go around town!"

Alessandra smothered a half laugh but still gave me a shove.

It was a bittersweet situation. Loving each other at different times and continuing to desire one another without having the will or the courage to really try again.

"I have to talk to you." Alina's voice had an urgency about it that made me forget our differences. That's the way it worked between us, or maybe it was just the way it worked for me.

Despite all the spite and resentment, I couldn't help but love her, the way you love your brothers and sisters.

"What's wrong?"

"I can't tell you on the phone. I need to see you."

We met in the Valentino Park, in the botanical garden, where you forget you're in the city because the noise of the traffic is suffocated by the water flowing over the stones. People lie on the grass there to sunbathe or read. I've often chosen this spot in the park to take pictures of relaxed and happy faces. Human beings have a special light when they are in tune with the place they're in.

"I've had an argument with Ica." She said it with such sadness that for a moment I thought she was crying. "Sorry Alina, but you're always arguing." I meant it. They'd done nothing but argue for the past year. Alina had also turned up at my house one night because she had decided to leave her for good. Forgiveness had come after she had found a rose on the windscreen of her car. Those who find it hard to make up their minds always fall for the romanticism induced by clichés and Alina had gone back to Erica, sulking and determined to make her pay, but she'd gone back.

"No, this time it's really over. All she does is lie and spend all our money on cocaine. And now she's got to the point where she's glued to the bottle day and night."

"Have you stopped?"

"I can control it. I can handle myself."

"But how can she understand the difference if one day you do it with her and then the next day you tell her that you can't?"

"Whose side are you on?" Was she upset because I didn't agree with her or because she had realised how inconsistent she was? "I'm not on anyone's side, but if you call me to talk about what's going on, then I'm going to give you an opinion!" Or did she think that I was going to passively endure a long and tormented monologue about the sadness of her situation? "You know I always tend to sort out problems quickly!"

"Yes, I know, that's why I have to ask you if I can come and stay with you until I find somewhere to live."

13

Alessandra used a calm but violent technique to insult me. She had just started having counselling sessions with a psychologist who had brought her to the conclusion that she had to constructively explore my every action in such a way as to appear the victim of everything I did.

"I can't believe you didn't say anything to me before you said yes." She was sitting cross-legged on the bed, naked, with her head down and her hands abandoned on the sheet in front of her crossed ankles.

"Well, what was I supposed to do? Tell her I had to ask your permission first?" I couldn't see the problem and I was annoyed by her scolding.

"Come on, didn't you think I'd be upset at the thought that your ex is going to be sleeping here with you?"

"She's my friend. You can't possibly see her as my ex after all this time."

"So if I went to sleep at Celeste's, you'd be fine?" Irritating and manipulative.

"It's not the same thing. My relationship with Alina has changed from ex-girlfriend to friend over the years because we've kept on seeing each other. You and Celeste have never seen or heard from each other since you split up."

"So you aren't willing to admit that you could show a bit more respect?"

"There's nothing but friendship between me and Alina." Some bitchy little part of me made me continue "anyway, you and I aren't a couple. We see each other when we feel like it but it's not an exclusive relationship."

She looked like she'd been punched in the face.

"But I love you."

"I love you too, but we've already tried and we know it doesn't work."

She took a long, deep breath and rubbed her hands over her face as if she wanted to physically remove the sadness from her skin. Crawling towards me with a smile, she said "there is one thing that works, darling."

Our satisfied and exhausted embrace was always something indefinite in time and space. Inevitably, when I wanted to stay in that limbo where arguments don't matter, she would get up to go to for something to eat or drink, or to take a shower. If it was Alessandra that wanted to give in to her illusions, it was me who felt the need to do something else. Emotional disappointment was always lurking on one side or the other and this was an ugly truth that had to be faced.

My biology professor in high school had once told me about a horrible experiment on mice that had been connected to two electrodes. One gave sexual pleasure and the other provided food. The electrodes were activated directly by the mice, who all starved to death. Besides wondering what the use of an experiment like this was, and condemning its gratuitous evilness, I was wondering which mechanisms were activated by my relationship with Alessandra.

"What are you thinking about?" She was getting dressed to leave. We had instinctively assumed the behaviour of secret lovers, even though there was really no need for it. As if the heart were protecting itself, as if loneliness were building itself up. Women hurt each other with firm and implacable kindness, leaving no room for interpretation. Women love each other until the dramatic end because they need some sensational reason to actually go, to give up that treasure they've so carefully loved and nurtured. Because we can never believe that all our love has gone to waste and because we can't cope with the knowledge that we can cause so much pain to someone we've loved. Even if we're no longer in love with them, we love them in a different dimension, unfathomable by those who are insensitive, amplified and multiplied by female empathy.

"I'm thinking about mice."

For a moment she stood motionless looking at me staring seriously at her.

She decided to laugh, to play the part of the girl I'd met four years before. She decided to be easy-going, airheaded and careless.

"Mice? I was hoping you were thinking of something a bit more glamorous and sensual, sweetheart!" She kissed me, holding my face with her hands. Moving her lips closer to my ear she kept her tone cheerful but I could feel the tears flowing down her face. Were they mine or hers?

"Well my love, I have to go. I've got things to do and so have you. Thinking about mice seems pointless to me. I think it would be better to focus on all the things that life can give us."

Was it a wonderful goodbye or a last attempt at putting things right?

I had just woken up and could hear sounds coming from the kitchen. The dogs were sleeping happily at the foot of the bed. Alina was making breakfast. The smell of coffee, the morning news on television and that nasty weather jingle.

Alina had been staying at my house for two weeks and from the second day on, I felt like I had gone on a journey through time. We had immediately plunged into our routine as a couple and I was choking while Alina seemed to think that it was the expression of a sacred scripture which indicated us as the chosen ones.

"Good morning." People shouldn't talk in the morning. People shouldn't talk to me in particular.

"Why do you get up so early?" But most importantly, why did she wake me and the dogs?

"I feel like I'm wasting time when I'm asleep."

"I feel like you're stealing my sleep."

"I've got your bath ready. I've already finished. I'll call into the supermarket for water on my way home, but you remember to call the girls for dinner tonight."

I kept opening doors looking for coffee cups. Alina opened the one where I used to keep the plates and held one out to me. The biscuits had ended up in the place that belonged to the herbal teas and the napkins had probably been abolished because I couldn't find them anywhere.

In just one second, I was drowning in an old nightmare. When I opened the wardrobe to look for some clean towels, I noticed her clothes next to mine. My primal instinct for survival drove me back to the kitchen.

"Have you found somewhere to live?"

"I'm going to see a place this afternoon but it's in an area I don't really like."

"I wouldn't be too fussy if I were you."

"Are you throwing me out?"

"No, I'm trying to save our friendship. We broke up because we weren't a good match."

"We broke up because you were whoring around."

And in a flash, we were back to square one. "How far away do I have to go? I don't expect to get back with you, but why do you have to be so categorical?"

"Because I love you and won't let us be forced into rebuilding a relationship which is fine the way it is and which I care about, due to something that would be a poor copy of what has already ended badly once."

That day Alina signed the contract for the first flat she saw.

14

The bar was empty that evening. The buffet offered a wide choice, particularly because I was the only one who could enjoy it.

"How come this huge crowd tonight?"

Emma threw a napkin holder at me which I dodged by pure chance. "There's a concert in the park just out the back, it's hot and everybody wants to be outside."

"Let's call a few friends so we don't waste the food." Linda seconded my proposal immediately. Emma gave in due to numerical inferiority. In any case, I'd already started sending texts.

I was supposed to be seeing Silvia that night. I'd met her years before in a club but nothing had really happened because I'd just met Alessandra. I met Silvia again through work. I was in charge of taking photos of the interiors of a hotel and she was in charge of creating the website. Emma had invited all her suitors and it seemed logical to lower the shutters and have a private party. Erica had come too, with my sister's friends. Shared interests lead very different people to weave unlikely relationships.

Linda was unusually euphoric and was drinking like a fish, despite the fact she wasn't eating anything.

The music was soft and a slow game of seduction between Silvia and me was making the evening interesting. She kept asking me to leave and I kept delaying so I could enjoy the wait. Erica was very quiet and not particularly involved in what was going on. She was pretending to mourn a loss that she didn't really feel but which allowed her to play a grieving version of herself that was sufficient to justify the abuse of drugs and alcohol. All that was left of her and Alina was anger, in both of them.

"I have to tell you something!" Linda was obviously drunk. Her white face framed by very blonde hair was almost ethereal. She stood up to climb on one of the wooden tables as if it were a podium, falling ruinously backwards. She laughed happily and unwittingly as Emma made a mental note to fire her.

"Linda maybe you should eat something."

"Only if you make me a sandwich. I'm always the one waiting on the tables so tonight you can do it for me."

After giving Silvia a kiss, I went to the kitchen to make the sandwich for Linda, who followed me shortly afterwards.

She was wrecked.

"What do you want in your sandwich?" I had a slice of bread in my right hand and a knife in my left hand, waiting for her to choose between mayonnaise or mustard. With my arms open and the bread in my hand I was waiting for Linda to tell me what to do and instead she wrapped herself around me in a sudden and clumsy kiss. Caught unawares, I tried to push her away with my body but only succeeded in creating a sort of sensual dance because my hands were full. Applause accompanied by the voice of Silvia pronouncing the word "congratulations" with each clap of her hands, made Linda stop. Silvia left and Linda got someone to come and pick her up. "God you're stupid. Don't go telling me you hadn't noticed that Linda had a soft spot for you?" Emma laughed like crazy while I was still trying to figure out what had happened.

"How was I supposed to notice?" Linda was married and had a little boy, and all she did was talk about her family. Had my lesbian radar stopped working? Erica, who had broken her silence, came up to me with a glass of vodka. "Interesting evening. You looked like Jesus with arms outstretched and bread in your hand." She was laughing too. Everybody was laughing.

Why did I always find myself in situations that made me guilty when I wasn't guilty at all?

The next group decision to continue the evening in a nearby club convinced us to walk there, taking some bottles of booze with us, to avoid driving. We had all agreed apart from Erica, who calmly and with unpredictable lucidity accompanied our night-time stroll in her car at walking pace.

I met everyone at the club. Alina was there too but when she realised that Erica was with us, she quickly took off.

"Hello gorgeous. The usual?" Katia the bartender held out a neat vodka and winked at me. Did I really want to live like this?

Erica was too close to me, like a predator ready to take advantage the moment I let my guard down, so I began looking around for an excuse to get away. Alina was near the cloakroom, about to leave and throwing me one of her accusing glances, Emma was dancing with her friend Tito next to the DJ while she was checking up on me, Katia the bartender was going on her break, so I turned to abandon Erica and join her. Then who should appear in front of me but Ada. Instinctively I shook my head like I wanted to tune in my brain.

I didn't think I'd had so much to drink that I could be hallucinating.

"You don't look very well."

"What are you doing here?"

"One of our friends has just graduated and we're celebrating."

"Have you become one of those people who speak about themselves in the plural form?"

"And what about you? Have you become a drunk who slurs her words when she's out?"

"Why didn't you tell me you were coming?"

Silence. Ada kissed me on the cheek and then went back to her friends with a look that left no room for me to follow her.

"Ica get me out of here."

"Where do you want to go?" Erica was looking at me with a sort of victory in her eyes. That light that illuminates a hunter who has spent hours waiting and can finally see his prey wandering close to the trap.

This detail brought me back to reality.

"Nowhere. I've changed my mind."

"As you wish your majesty!" She was annoyed and looking at me as if I'd just broken her new toy.

"Sorry Erica, I didn't mean to be rude." I said it politely while trying to locate Ada and her group of friends.

"Don't be, let's just go. I've had enough of it here." She sounded just like a spoilt child.

"You've got a car. Why don't you leave?"

"You're so nice Sonia! I was trying to be kind since you have to walk home." You could sense the childish spite behind the hurt expression.

"Thanks, but I'd rather walk."

Erica gave me a military-style salute followed by her middle finger as she walked away.

I felt Ada's presence behind me before she started talking.

"I must say, I was hoping to meet you in better company. Who was that?" The judgment and the tone of mockery were probably due to Erica's physical appearance which Ada, being an aesthete and a lover of beauty, couldn't help but mention.

"Alina's ex-girlfriend. I still can't believe you came to Turin without telling me."

"I would have told you tomorrow. I just decided right at the last minute to come up with Augusto in the car."

"Hello beautiful!" Augusto lifted me up by the waist and after twirling me around a couple of times, squeezed me to him the way only he had permission to do.

"Hi Ago, how are you? Why the surprise? Why didn't you let me know you were coming?"

"I had to tell you in person," his eyes were gleaming. At least I was going to get some good news. "I'm getting married to the woman of my dreams in three weeks!"

Ada smiled as he placed his hand on her shoulder and, at that point, I really did want everything to be a hallucination

"Aren't you going to say anything? You look frozen."

More than frozen, I was terrified, but I definitely wasn't going to let them see.

"Congratulations?" It was too much for me to pretend to be happy about such a badly matched couple.

"I can't do it! Fuck congratulations!" Before Augusto could answer me, I began to blurt out all my disappointment: "how do you think you can build a happy life with someone who's always treated you like a doormat? You used to tease me about Alessandra and then you get married to a lesbian who's only looking for someone to join her on her adventures?" I was in full swing now.

"And you? Since when have you needed someone to cover for you? I thought you'd reached a balance between one flirt and the next."

Ada burst out laughing and stretched her left hand out towards Augusto with her palm facing upwards. Fingers moving to claim what was due.

"Ada said you'd fall for it, but I didn't think she'd even get the sequence of insults right."

Augusto gave Ada fifty euros and she winked at me. "You know I wouldn't look for the only cover I need in a man. By the way, Augusto really is getting married but to Lidia.

The girl we've come to Turin for."

I'd made a right fool of myself. "I don't know whether to be happy for you or to insult you both again."

"Tell me that you'll come to my wedding and take the photos and then you can insult me."

"Of course I will. How could I refuse after the uterine monologue I just put you through?"

"Good!" Augusto wrapped Ada and me in a satisfied hug, squeezing us tight "now let's just enjoy ourselves."

We danced all night and then went to have breakfast in a bakery in the centre of town, which had been giving a semblance of sobriety to the people of the night that I loved being part of, for years, with its freshly baked pizzas and croissants.

I was sitting on the step of a shop that was shut, watching Emma's carefree expressions, Ada's satisfied air and Augusto's explosive happiness, and wondering what the secret to living in a permanent state of grace and inner satisfaction was.

Suddenly, that morning, as Ada sat right next to me, I realised how stupid I had been and smiled.

"Why the smile?"

"Write this down because you'll never hear me say it again: I'm sorry. You were right."

Ada sat motionless, staring at me without understanding.

"About what? And why are you saying sorry to me?"

"The truth always pays. The fact that you are honest with yourself, and especially with others, makes your relationships transparent. You don't expect anything and you don't create expectations in others. You live the people around you and you give yourself to them, the way you really are."

"Sonia, you sound like you're spouting a philosophy lesson or an episode in a television programme where at some point everyone starts crying and making their peace, and I must warn you that both options bore me to death."

She laughed, maybe a little embarrassed, but she had a light in her eyes that made me keep going.

"I'm just saying that you're right. You always were."

"Since when have we ever discussed the obvious?" She took my hand and kissed my lips gently.

"You and I will always be you and I."

"That's the first romantic thing you've said to me in nine years!"

Ours was a liberating laugh, an intimate peace. Ada needed to be told that she wasn't necessarily the one who was wrong and I needed to understand that I wasn't always right.

15

"Have we finished our journey in time?"

The wind has started blowing and it's time to go home. My bizarre afternoon with Angelica has come to an end. "We decided from the start to look back into the past, unless I'm mistaken."

"Yes, we did, but we also said that we would eventually come to some kind of conclusion."

"I suppose you aren't going to give me an answer even now." I watch her get up from her chair slowly and start to dismantle her stage. She puts the Tarot cards in the black velvet bag and then wraps it in a white cloth.

She takes out a dark bag, which is so worn you can't tell what colour it is, and puts the bag of cards inside it. She acts as if she's alone and it doesn't seem like she's going to say a word. She just keeps on getting ready to leave. "So is this where we say goodbye?" I feel embarrassed at this point, like when you realise that you are the last table in a restaurant and the staff discreetly start letting you know that it's time to go.

"You've been an interesting subject but you still haven't answered my question."

"I still think you should review the dynamics of your reading."

"You said you'd relive it all without changing a thing because you're afraid of losing what you've achieved. What is it?"

"Freedom."

She shakes her head and laughs as though I've fallen into her trap.

"She's dead and you'll never be able to change her mind. She died convinced that you were guilty." "What that's got to do with it?"

"This is the point."

Standing opposite each other. It seems like a duel that I appear to be losing. I don't want to play this game anymore.

"Why don't I come back tomorrow and we'll dig a bit deeper."

"You wouldn't find me, and it's not worth it anyway. You won't understand what I have to say now, only when you start really living."

"Just say it so we can say goodbye."

Angelica takes two steps towards me and I make an effort not to give in to the impulse to retreat. I don't know why, but I'm agitated as if she might be going to say something that will upset me.

"You've had a number of women who have loved you and who, at some point, you've left. You have revolutionised your life every four years, throwing yourself into a new relationship that was destined to follow a pattern that is deep within you. They were all doomed from the start."

"If you're going to rattle off some cliché, forget it. I'm not homosexual because I had a conflictual relationship with my mother."

"Of course not! If that was the reason, we'd all be homosexual. Haven't you ever read anything on psychology?"

Why don't I end the conversation now and leave? I'm going to say goodbye now.

"Just wait a minute and then I'll let you go." I start to panic! How does she do it?

"You've learned a lot from the relationships you've had and I mean all of them, not just the romantic ones. Now you have all the tools you need to break away from your pattern and today you've managed to relive things that will seem clearer to you." Angelica fiddles with her bag and grasps the table.

"I'll be here when you've worked it out, not when you come looking for me. It'll be about a year before we meet again but it will only happen if you use all the tools you have to get out of the little world you live in, to enter a universe of possibilities and really start living your life." I almost expect her to bow at this point, but she turns and walks away without looking back.

She has left me standing here like an idiot. Because that's what I am, of course. An expensive and useless afternoon spent with a madwoman who talks like a box of pessimistic fortune cookies.

Now I'm going have to run to Emma's. I'd better not tell her about Angelica because she could go on making fun of me for years.

16

It's been two weeks and I still wake up thinking about the fortune-teller's words. Today is Augusto's big day and although technically I'm working, I can't wait to see him finally happy.

My dogs watch me having breakfast, looking like they're concentrating on trying to move the biscuits on the table with the power of thought. I let them out into the garden before I go so I can take them to my neighbour who looks after them whenever I have to spend the whole day away. Why does the phone always have to ring just before I get in the car?

"Hi, where are you?" It's a question that always annoys me! "I'm going to Ago's wedding."

She seems to be waiting for something. Lately my phone calls with Alessandra are long and silent, a boring and embarrassed parenthesis that I can't be bothered with anymore. "I haven't got time to listen to your silence on the phone because I can't find my earphones." "God you're so mean, I just wanted to ask you how are and if you're going to drop by when you're done."

I don't really feel like it, but if I tell her that, she'll try to convince me, "Of course! I'll call you when I'm about to leave." That way I can send her a text with an excuse and that'll solve the problem.

"I'm glad! Have a good day and enjoy yourself darling."

The bride and groom are glowing and the guests are bored stiff because the string quartet engaged by way of musical entertainment has just six pieces in its repertoire, which it keeps repeating endlessly with no light relief at all. I'm going to kill her.

"What are you so mad about?" Ada, with her glass of white wine, laughs shamelessly in my face.

"I'm impaled next to a tripod, taking fixed shots in which the only thing that changes are the zombies in front of the lens!" All because the bride's mother doesn't like the idea of a photo reporting style commemoration of the day but wants a traditional album.

"They look like funeral remembrance cards."

"It's worse than that: it's like a horror film featuring zombies all dressed up in their Sunday best. I'm going to make Ago suffer for this!"

"Don't be angry. To be honest, I'm glad you're not too busy to listen to me." There she goes, ready to seize any opportunity to avoid being bored. "Admit it. You're trying it on with me because you haven't found anyone else interesting to play with."

"You're dreadful. But you're right." She guzzles the wine down in one "And what's wrong with that? You told me that I was right all along, so let's have some fun." Ok, the assistant is being paid just to stand there holding a cable because I don't know what else to make him do. He can do what I'm doing.

"Excellent idea! Let's start by going and getting some more wine." She looks almost shocked and I don't know whether it's because she didn't expect me to say yes or because she'd only been joking. Perhaps I should clarify things because I don't want to find myself in a horrendously awkward situation later. "It'll be nice to play with you knowing that we can push ourselves to the limit without going all the way." She takes my hand like an excited little girl who wants to show me her presents under the tree. "Now I know you're the woman of my dreams." The bride and groom must have escaped and the relatives are still queuing up, as if they were in the post office, to be immortalised with false expressions in a family picture.

We cross our glasses and make a toast, gazing into each other's eyes.

The party is basically over and it's time to put all the equipment away. I don't trust the assistant sent by the temping agency so I do it myself. Ada is on the phone to one of her love interests. I forgot to text Alessandra.

I rummage through my bag looking for my phone. Twenty-two missed calls and four texts.

I'd better read them before I call her. "Babe, it's gone four, what time will you be here?" I sense that the insults are going to start now. "I should have known. You're such a bitch! Why can't you answer me!?"

Should I call her? While I'm putting the equipment away the phone rings again and it's her, but I don't want to answer. I did tell her I'd be working.

"Who aren't you answering?" Ada was watching me without me even noticing.

"Alessandra. I told her I would stop by after the wedding just to end a conversation, but I forgot to tell her I couldn't. So she's furious now and she's called me so many times."

"Did she know you'd be working?"

"Yes, of course."

"Call her and ask her if anything has happened and try to sound worried. Then, when she says no, that's your cue to lose your temper. And you tell her that having fun is one thing but working is another." "I don't know whether to tell you that you're evil or give you a kiss."

"Kiss me while you tell me I'm evil and we'll both be happy." She winked but the glimmer in her eyes was pretty clear. We had teased each other all afternoon and while neither of us had any intention of retracing our footsteps, it's hard to tell your body that the heart and mind have moved off in a different direction.

Alessandra took a second to answer "do you realise how you treat me? I'm not some whore you can call whenever you want!" "Good. Now I know you're alive and kicking. I've just finished work and didn't have time to text you. I was worried about all the calls because I thought something had happened to you. But it's always just the fact that you're spoiled that causes problems."

"So now it's my fault Sonia?"

"No, it's my fault because I try to make you happy every day but it's impossible."

"Are you coming over? We can talk about it face to face." Her tone of voice is different, Alessandra never tries to drag on arguments, only to make peace as quickly as possible.

"I can't" Ada watches me, touching her lips with a finger, "I have to go home. I left the dogs with my neighbour and she has to go out". Ada kisses my neck while she caresses my back. "Well I'll come over to yours then". I don't know whether I want to continue this game with Ada but I definitely know that seeing Ale would be a bad idea.

"No, I'm tired, I'll see you tomorrow."

"Congratulations, your self-control was impeccable." Ada whispered in my ear before walking away. "I'm going to Ago's mum and dad's house to get my bags. I've got to catch a train this evening. Will you give me a lift?"

In my car, with Ada's hand on mine, sitting outside the station, I felt as though I'd travelled back in time, just like I had felt with Angelica. Except that now the memories are made of flesh and blood and the emotions are alive not sweetened by a comfortable point of view to avoid getting involved.
"By the way, I love you" she said it with a melancholy but amused smile.
"Right, you and I will always be you and I." I'm sincere and not in the least bit embarrassed.
"No Sonia, you don't get it. I really do love you."
Now I am embarrassed. "When you spoke to me three weeks ago and told me I was right, I thought about it and, in actual fact, I was always wrong."
What's happening? Ever since I talked to that psychic, things have escalated. The clearer an idea I have about things, the more the people around me are losing their bearings. It's like I've woken up from a dream and they're still living it.
"Ada, I don't think you're being serious! You just told me that you were wrong. Are you okay? Should I take you to see a doctor or an exorcist?" "Stop being daft. You know I'm not all that keen on life as a couple, but I've only ever really expressed myself with you. Every time I flirted with someone, I knew I wanted to go home to you." She squeezes my hands as if she needs to muster up the courage to continue, "it wasn't you I didn't like, it was my ego that wouldn't let me tell you how much I wanted you." There. Now I'm sure she's under the effect of some substance or other. "What are you talking about,

and why?" It's been years since we first met. "Because I couldn't make you understand how inexperienced I was and the pleasure I felt with you was so intense that it made me compete with you. I didn't want to play the part of the innocent little girl."

I can't help laughing. "Sorry to laugh, don't take it badly. I adore you. You are one of the most important people in my life Ada, but your inexperience was completely obvious, and what does it matter in a relationship anyway?"

"I know that. At least now I do. At the time, though, I was in a perverse state of mind and I just want to apologise." She kisses me with a profound sense of calm that has nothing to prove. "I have to thank you too because, by talking so sincerely, you gave me the courage to do the same." I'm baffled but also happy because she seems to have really lifted a weight off her heart.

"Now come on, or I'll miss my train and keep making a fool of myself."

"You couldn't make a fool of yourself even if you tried."

Another kiss prompted by the heart's need to reconnect with a body that it has loved.

"The Intercity train for Venezia Mestre is departing from platform 15." We're telling each other everything, laughing like two 15-year-olds. Being able to completely relax with someone is incredibly important.

As she gets on the train, she stops and, with her worldly, femme-fatale expression, says "I love you and you know it, but I'm not going to chase you. I'll let the others do that. I'll wait for you until I don't feel like waiting anymore." A wink, a blown kiss and then she vanishes into the carriage.

As I watch the train leave the station, I ask myself what has actually happened. Why have we never opened our hearts before? Maybe because it's too risky when you can still get hurt? Meanwhile, I'd better get out of here so I don't look like a desperate woman staring at the empty tracks. Since my inner journey with Angelica, I tend to become lost, motionless, in my thoughts.

I only told Elena about Angelica. Obviously she laughed but she also decided, since she's going to be spending about six months here for work, to find her and get some answers of her own.

"You don't get it! You'll never get any answers from her."

"She'd better tell me something."

I look at the clock and I realise it's very late. The road I'm driving along is semi-deserted and Ada's perfume is still hanging in the car.

After I get home, I cuddle up on the couch with Oscarina, my lovely old dog who begs for biscuits, and with India, the little black sister I adopted for Oscarina, who didn't appreciate my gesture at all. She puts up with her to please me, while India loves us both unconditionally.

Right now, I'm enjoying the happiness, while I'm looking for a film to watch.

Elena will be in town from tomorrow so it won't be easy to enjoy an evening of calm and silence.

17

"You should have told me." The nurse is giving me a dirty look because I'm being particularly unpleasant and, since I walked into the room, I've done nothing but moan. I can't stand it when people hide the truth from me with the excuse of "I didn't want to worry you". Worry is an essential element that alerts our brain and our soul to something. Otherwise, bad news rains down on you like a cold shower. "What difference would it have made? And you're always so annoying when you try to take control of everything and sort everything out." "Just because you've decided to do something stupid doesn't mean that we all have to go along with it." "Sonia, if you want to be of any help stop taking your bad temper out on me. I'm not dying!" Stop whingeing and get used to it because I've made my mind up" She looks at me and smiles. "I've always wanted to do it" Elena had told me she would be coming back and staying for six months, missing out a lot of details. She told me she'd been thinking about it for a long time and had decided to have a breast enhancement. A generous D cup to fit in with the way she saw herself. "We even used to talk about it at school, remember? When they start sagging, it'll be time to have them inflated."

"But not because you fall in love with a woman who forces you to do it."

"She's not forcing me. She just said that she likes big breasts."

"You're right, nutcase! When you're done here, where do we want to go?"

"It really turns me on when you get all forceful." She laughs light-heartedly and I don't know how she does it, but her calmness has always been contagious. "I'd say you could take me to find your fortune-teller. I'm really curious!"

"I'm not sure we'll find her". What I really mean is that I'm not sure I want to feed Elena to Angelica or vice versa. I'm laughing at the thought of the scene. "At least tell me what she made you do. Since you met her you seem to be even more thoughtful and, in your case, that's serious because you were already an intimist."

"She left me speechless because she told me that I had thought my mother's death would release me, and I hadn't told her anything. She couldn't have known."

She thinks as she furtively points to the nurse's backside. "Good. That means you've stumbled across someone who knows what she's doing." There was some logic to what she was saying. "From then on, almost nothing. She hinted at things but I mostly went on a journey inside myself."

She nodded, smiling and stroking her bracelet which had belonged to her mother, who had died ten years earlier. "She used to love the Tarot cards, you know, and sometimes she'd take me to this woman's house and they'd spend hours talking and squabbling. From what you say, it sounds like an evolutionary reading that pushes you to probe your conscience, understand yourself and live a better life."

"You could be right. But I'm not sure I've benefited from it."

"You told me you solved a lot with Ada." I snort and sit next to her. "Yes, I did. But she told me that she loves me and that she'll wait for me for as long as she feels like it." Elena rests her head on me "Oh my God! You must be really unforgettable in bed!"

She makes fun of me like she always has, from that first day when we both caught each other staring a little too closely at the nude model at school.

"At the end of the day, it doesn't matter who's upset now. The important thing is that it's all over and done with. So you can both get on with your lives."

"You sound like a Zen teacher. Are they standard accessories that come with the tits or is it the idea of becoming a big-boobed woman that obliges you to express introspection and intellect?"

"Did I ever tell you that if you weren't my friend, I'd marry you?"

"Since when have you been so melodramatic? Come on, hurry up. When we get out, we're going to go and have a good time."

"I can't wait. Vodka, women and music like there's no tomorrow." We laugh so much that the nurse orders us to be quiet and sends me to wait outside.

On my way out, I think that maybe I shouldn't be going along with her in this whole thing, even though I appreciate her courage.

Elena has been with me through all the great events of my life. My bright and edgy confidante has never agreed with me simply because she's my friend so I can't judge her, because she doesn't deserve it, but I have every intention of making fun of her.

Preparations for my birthday party are in full swing at Emma's bar and, although I'm not supposed to know anything about it, every year the attempt at keeping it a surprise fails miserably. As I drink my coffee, I try not to lift my head up from the newspaper so as not to embarrass Linda who hasn't spoken to me since the evening of the kiss, apart from to ask me what I want to order, pretending that she's forgotten everything. I agree with her and put up the same pretence, avoiding even the slightest eye contact so as not to trigger temptation.

Elena won't be there because she's going to be spending ten days with her dad in the mountains and I, like every other year, would love to go on holiday, to celebrate the milestone looking at something new.

"What are you thinking about?"

"That I want to go on holiday for my birthday." Emma makes a face at me, horrified at the very thought. My sister is a creature of habit and doesn't have a good relationship with humanity. She has built her life to suit her own standards, not what is universally acknowledged as socially acceptable, and she's completely satisfied with it. A bit gloomy and lonely, but happy.

"I suppose asking you to come with me is out of the question."

"Are you mad? Ask Alessandra. She can't wait, if you ask me."

"Not on your life. We've left each other too many times for me to bear another one." "But you aren't even together"

"I know, but every time we end up in bed or even just go to see a film, we fall back into the same old habits."

"What about going on your own?"

It's not such a bad idea, but I'd disappoint everyone if I missed the party, everyone except Emma, who, just like every other year, offers me much more interesting ideas than a boring surprise party.

I'm always late when I have to catch a plane and I end up running at breakneck speed to get to the boarding gate in time. As I'm panting for breath, I realise that I should do more sport and I think about how many times Elena has run with me in the same situation, overtaking me by miles and laughing like crazy. It'll soon be me that's laughing when she's running. The flight attendant asks me for my documents and looks at me, alarmed, as if I were about to die in front of her.

I gesture to reassure her and try to talk, but I give up. I'd better start running again when I get back from Barcelona, otherwise I'll become one of those old women who gets breathless climbing the stairs.

I love flying and I love the feeling of travelling all that distance between the earth and the sky filled with anticipation. It seems so much more exciting, being a little closer to the stars. I sit in my seat and pull out a book that I bought last week, on impulse, by an author I don't know, on a subject I know nothing about. As I get ready to start reading, I notice the feet of the person who's going to sit in the seat next to me. I'm not the only one who shows up at the last minute, then. Raising my head to say hello politely, who should I see in front of me but Erica, who looks at me in disbelief.

"Hi. What are you doing here?" What a stupid question. "I'm checking the seats to see if they're comfortable. What do you think I'm doing? I'm going to Barcelona for my birthday!"

"On your own?" She sounds more embarrassed than surprised.

"What's wrong with that?" All I want to do is change flight and destination but it's too late now and I put the book back into my bag.

"It just seems strange that someone like you should be going to celebrate their birthday alone, that's all."

"Someone like me? Forget it. It looks like you're on your own too."

"I am, but I'm joining Lara and Mina. They're flying from Rome and we're meeting up at the hotel."

"I don't think I know them, do I?" Erica shakes her head. "Lara's my ex, my first love. We're still friends. I told you about her once but you probably don't remember. Mina's one of her friends."

"It seems as though you're still very much into Lara."

"Yes and no. I'll never stop loving her, but I could never live with her." We lesbians are so boring. We all say the same thing. My male friends are much more honest when they tell me "I wouldn't mind giving her one but I don't want any hassle" instead of being so wistful and deep.

Erica looks different. Her hairstyle enhances her instead of hiding her and she's wearing contact lenses. Apparently, she's also discovered hair removal and, while her style is still masculine, she now has a feminine touch. Instead of looking like a straight man, she now just looks like a gay man. "You look much better." I say it instinctively, without thinking. "Why? Did I look awful before?" She laughs, sniffing. "Don't worry, I know all about what Alina said about me and I know I don't turn any heads, but it doesn't matter, I'm happy the way I am." I still get the feeling she has an agenda.

"Can I be honest with you?"

"Of course."

"I get the impression you're flirting with me. Am I wrong?" "No, you aren't, but you've never given me the chance to tell you anything about myself." Here we go. It's going to be a very long flight. "There's never really been a chance. But it's also because I'm not interested in anything but friendship at the moment." Erica looks at me as if I'm mad.

"But every time you go into a club, you leave with someone new!"

"Why is it that people seem to have so much fun spying on my sex life?"

When it's time for take-off, Erica turns as white as a corpse and then red as a traffic light. "Are you frightened of flying?" She nods and grips the armrest tightly as she closes her eyes. Hopefully she'll stay that way until Barcelona. At least I'll be able to read.

"Don't think you're going to get away with it. I'll be fine as soon as we're up." Is everybody clairvoyant now?

18

The Barcelona sun is shining, making up for the two-hour flight spent justifying my complete disinterest in Erica. I don't understand why she's so insistent, especially because she told me that she's not really attracted to me, just curious. Basically, she's just bored and this is one of reasons I made sure I lost her at the airport. The descriptions of the two girls she's going to be meeting aren't very encouraging, so I decided to hurry off to my hotel and then to seek immediate refuge on a quiet beach.

It's not like me to spend my birthday alone but I feel unusually happy and satisfied. Staring romantically at the horizon without having any questions to answer or things to do to please someone gives me an amazing sense of gratification that calms me down.

"I knew I'd find you here." I'm so disappointed that anger can't even creep in through the sadness. I really need to be alone, to take off all the masks I wear, consciously or otherwise, to reconsider Angelica's words and maybe to deal with my thoughts about my mother. One thing is certain: I've done everything I possibly can in my life to fill it up with activities and people so I don't have to listen to myself. "You didn't think I'd let you spend your birthday without me!" Alessandra standing in front of me against the sun looks like a super heroine wrapped in rays of light. "That was the idea. I also told you that I wanted to spend some time away from everyone and everything." The feeling of sadness is fading and quickly becoming a sense of anger.

"And I meant it! You're intrusive and asphyxiating Ale!" I get up, feeling like I've been violated and with growing resentment which amazes me and makes me determined at the same time. "I have no intention whatsoever of spending the next three days with you just to avoid hurting you. I'm going somewhere else and I'd appreciate it if you wouldn't waste any more of my time trying to convince me to change my mind."

"You are so horrible to me! I'm here now. Can't we just spend three days together? Is it too much to ask?" I feel my blood go cold. Without knowing it, Alessandra has opened my eyes in an instant. Her request summarises my entire life and the nature of my frustrations. Her disappointment, the driving force behind my actions, and my instinct not to want those I love to think that I am a bad person or that I don't do everything I can to protect the relationship, are the cause of all my choices. And all this is the expression of a series of self-sabotage attacks that have prevented an evolution of which I was perhaps afraid.

"No Ale, we aren't going to spend three days together. I'm sorry if you feel hurt but it's not my fault and I'm not taking responsibility for it." "You've come with someone else, haven't you?" Accusingly, she starts looking around as if she expects to see a girl come out of the sand proving my guilt.

"Think what you want. I imagine it's easier to think that I have something to hide than believe that I don't want to spend my time with you. You're the one who's making a scene, when you're the one who's in the wrong. Because you're the one who's forced your presence on me. I didn't sneak away with an excuse, I told you I was going away on my own because I wanted to go on holiday with only myself for company." Alessandra looks at me silently but there is something in her expression that I can't quite put my finger on. Anger mixed with disappointment. Then a sudden, violent slap interrupts my thoughts. "You're so manipulative. You almost succeeded in making me feel guilty. You really are a horrible person, Sonia." I'm still dazed by the slap and I can't understand what has triggered Alessandra's exaggerated reaction.

"I see you got your girlfriend to join you in the end." Erica appears from behind me wearing black shorts and with a towel over her shoulder. Alessandra had clearly seen her long before I knew she was there. Once again, I've fallen victim to a situation in which I'm being blamed for nothing. Once again, I have to pray for my innocence to be accepted.

"With that? You left me at home and lied to me to spend time with that?" I almost burst out laughing, although I don't know whether to be angrier with the one who seems to do everything in her power to ruin my life or with the other who says she loves me but then proves that she knows absolutely nothing about me.

"Who's she calling "that"?"

The question I'm asking is, why are they both addressing me as if I have the answers?

Like in the best screenplays, Alessandra turns towards me, blocking out Erica "now tell her to go away and not speak to me."

I can see some kids not far away laughing and pointing at our little drama, egging each other on to come forward. The empty beer bottles around their towels immediately tell me it's time to go "Let's stop making a show of ourselves and get out of here."

But Alessandra is hysterical, "No! No way! You give me an answer now. I don't care if I'm showing you up. She can go if she wants." I look at Erica who is following my gaze in the direction of the group nearby and nods "don't worry petal, I was already going. I don't want to get involved in problems that don't even have anything to do with me." She walks straight towards the kids and with a few moves, pulls something out of her bag. With a friendly laugh, she somehow manages to divert their attention, walking away with them. When you're used to going to clubs as yourself and you're homosexual you can decide to behave in two ways when faced with the problems that always arise. The first is to challenge them but this always creates confusion and is potentially dangerous. The second is to anticipate them: those who want to cause a disturbance usually have standard attitudes that you learn to spot immediately and then you become capable of nipping everything in the bud.

Alessandra seems calmer, just because she's won, beating Erica, but I can't help thinking about the fact that the stupid woman has gone somewhere with those kids just to help me. Did she lure them away with cocaine? If that's the case, what's going to happen when they've smoked it? "Are you listening to me?" Alessandra is looking at me as if she doesn't know me and I realise in that precise instant how true it is. "I'm not listening to you because I'm worried about Erica. She went away with a bunch of people who wanted to mess with us and you didn't even notice." This time I see the slap coming and do nothing to avoid it. As her eyes betray all the resentment she feels towards me, I look at her face and see the expressions of my mother, Alina, Ada and all those people who, over the years, have put me in a position to try to fix something that I haven't broken, something that I am supposed to have destroyed or perhaps glued clumsily together, assigning me the role of showing how much I love and how sorry I am. My mistake in consenting to this trap lies in the heart, which requires a minimum of energy to make someone happy. It makes you believe that you can pretend to be guilty in order to ease the pain that that person thinks you have caused them. It tells you that even if you spend your life being forgiven for something that you haven't done, you can resist by virtue of the fact that you know the truth and that, despite everything, you have decided to make their vision more important. By avoiding being proud, I've damaged my ego. Without saying a word, I look at her and something in my expression must have awakened similarly constructive reflections in her too, because she turns around and begins to walk quickly and proudly along the beach. This time I get the feeling that the story with Alessandra really is over and, even if it isn't over for her, my awareness pushes me to look further ahead. I've been looking for Erica for over an hour now and I doubt I'll find her. She isn't answering her phone and I realise I don't know which hotel she's booked into. Maybe it's another one of those situations where I'd be better off staying out of the way. I find it hard to let things run their course and have the extreme presumption that I can influence them somehow. I'm so stupid. I'm crying and I don't even know why. The evening wind is starting to feel harsh and not pleasant at all. Tourists are ready for the long night, wandering around trying to decide where to eat and, as I walk to my hotel, I think about the fact that, at midnight, I will be celebrating the first birthday on which I have finally realised that I have grown up.

19

Erica is fine, even if that's the only information she has given me, in a text, a few hours after my arrival at the hotel. As always, she becomes cryptic and uncommunicative after using drugs. She talked to me quite a lot about her addiction on the plane, describing it more as a life choice than a mistake, and despite all my objections, I was unable to convince her to the contrary. I feel much better after a shower and dinner in a little restaurant in the centre of town. A celebration of grilled vegetables and rice that I managed to order in my dreadful Spanish from a waiter who had a good laugh with me about something that probably neither of us fully understood. "Did you go to celebrate your birthday or commit suicide in solitude?" Elena's voice on the phone is loud and piercing and I can hear voices and music as if she were at a concert. "Where are you, the stadium?" She laughs cheekily, relaxed and happy, and I wonder if she has corrupted her extremely serious father or if she has already abandoned him. "I'm at your birthday party stupid! I wanted to surprise you, but you surprised me!" I can't believe it. "Instead of surprising me, why don't you all just state your intentions?" My tone is one of genuine horror. I'm sad. The intent when I left had been different, as had my mood. "Stop being a victim! I bet you're having a great time. I have to thank you because every woman in town is here and they're all devastated at your absence. Obviously, I'm more than willing to console them." "I don't have a hard time believing that, but I don't think any of them are your type." Only she can cheer me up even when I'm feeling terrible. Even when I rushed to her house to tell her what had happened with my mother, she had simply shrugged her shoulders "so now you have a nice trauma with your mum that some idiot can use against you."

"What about you? How are you celebrating?"

137

"I've just finished eating and thought I'd go somewhere to drink a toast to myself and then go to bed." "When you come back to Italy, will you be going straight to an old people's home or have you decided to become a nun?"

"You don't have to be surrounded by people to have fun, you know"

"No, but you have to do something fun! You're doing something gloomy. It might be relaxing, but it definitely doesn't have much to do with the idea of celebrating."

I say nothing. The idea of being at the party doesn't appeal to me and even though I would have liked to see Elena, I'm glad I didn't stay. I know that what I want is to be on my own as much as possible. No more relationships that require emotional involvement or long-term promises. Better to give free rein to love that has a date of expiry. There's a curve that inevitably works its way towards the end and then turns the sentiment into something that leaves a trail of "I still love you", "I can't stand you but I can't stay away", "you're like a sister and I can't live without you" and an endless series of emotional adaptations for something that you feel has been lost. Falling in love again creates the urge to justify yourself and to think that the previous relationship was a mistake, an oversight and that this, on the other hand, is the right one. A perpetual cycle of hope that fills the soul with disappointments and defeats.

And while Emma and Elena are celebrating the funeral of my old life, letting go of everything that has slowed me down, with smiles and toasts, I celebrate my rebirth in complete harmony with my new self, with a glass of wine. "If we keep meeting like this, you'll think I'm stalking you."

"Oh so you aren't lying dead in an alleyway then!" I smile and free up the chair next to mine. Erica seems puzzled.

"How much have you had to drink?"

"A glass of wine, why?"

"You're never usually happy to see me and now you're even smiling!" She sits down and gestures to the waitress who nods and immediately brings her a glass of what looks like vodka.

"Do they know you?" She looks she feels at home. "I come here a lot and I'm thinking of moving here."

"How come?"

"Because if I stayed in Italy and stopped using drugs, I would have to prove to everyone that it's true, every day, and still be labelled as a cokehead." "Then we have to toast to two rebirths tonight, I'm glad you shared it with me."

"Now I can see why they all fall in love with you."

"Because I always find a reason to make a toast and smile?" Erica laughs while she pays for both of us, and I know by now that there's no point in trying to stop her. "That too, but I think it's the kind light in your eyes and the fact that standing next to you everything seems possible. Because you sincerely encourage, you're never in competition and you're full of energy that you use to help others." I feel a bit embarrassed because I have never seen myself through someone else's eyes before and the picture doesn't look as awful as I've always thought.

All I can say is "thank you", without adding anything else. It's not easy to embarrass me, but she just has. "And then you have this brazen sexual energy!" I burst out laughing at the natural ease with which she talks about topics that most people would find embarrassing.

"Don't laugh, it's true! There are urban legends passed from ex to ex about you!" Now she's clearly making fun of me, but the moment is almost as pleasant as those I've always spent with Elena. Once it becomes clear that a relationship can't evolve, the parties adapt naturally, following that original attraction, which we are used to confusing always and only as love or sex, expressing it in some other way. I can't wait to spend an evening with Erica and Elena together. Two different people with two complementary types of madness who both make me feel good for different reasons.

"Barcelona is a big city; how did you find me so easily?" "The city's big but Italians are sadly predictable, and we always end up in the same places." She pauses for a moment and then continues "your girlfriend is getting drunk in my hotel. I met her today when I left the beach and explained everything, once I managed to get her to listen to me." "I don't know whether to be happy. Now she's going to insist on spending all her time with me or getting me to forgive her." "If she does what I think she will to get you to forgive her then you'll end up celebrating your birthday properly and not like mad, lonely 80-year-old."

"Remind me to introduce you to my friend Elena when we get home, you suffer from the same form of madness."

"Alina told me about her, she always said she was beautiful but a bitch and that you were screwing her while you were still together."

"She's right about everything except my relationship with Elena. She's been my best friend since high school and no matter how explicitly we play around, there's never been anything between us."

"It's just as well. I don't want to have to compete with your ghost again."

"Look, I'm not introducing you to her to form a couple."

"You said she was beautiful, so I'll try to sleep with her anyway. If anything comes of it, then so much the better."

She stretches on the chair, smiling and twisting her lips to show me that she's joking "I also tried with Alessandra at the hotel but even though she was drunk she kept calling out your name". She's really on form. Too bad I didn't find out how nice she is before.

"Seriously, I told her I'd go out and look for you and that I'd bring you back, not to sort things out or to cause any more trouble, but to spend an evening together. She accepted immediately and was all smiles." That's just like her. She doesn't hold grudges and always puts the negative behind her.

Then suddenly I remember something "what happened to your ex and her friend?" Erica lowers her eyes imperceptibly but immediately resumes her cheerful tone "they decided to delay their departure for a couple of weeks at the last minute because of a problem at work. They know I come here a lot." I think I can see the hurt in her eyes but she doesn't seem to want to talk about it.

"Can I ask you a personal question?"

"Another one? Don't you ever mind your own business?"

"How did you get rid of those idiots today? I was worried sick." Erica laughs loudly "sometimes you're so naive. They weren't idiots, they were the friends I was going to meet when I bumped into you today."

"And here was I thinking you were being my hero and that you'd saved me for love."

"I did more than that partner, I calmed down the girlfriend so you can celebrate properly."

We go out and start walking towards the hotel, chatting and laughing, swapping past impressions of each other and forging one of those bonds that feels continuous.

When we reach the hotel, we see Alessandra running towards us because, just like an impatient little girl, she is sitting on the steps waiting for us. I think that, for the rest of my life, no matter what kind of relationship we have, I won't be able to stay angry with her for long. "I thought you'd abandoned me."

She hugs me, jumping into my arms and crossing her legs around my hips. "Can't you wait until you're in your room? Sonia, you must tell me how you do it because I'm starting to get seriously curious." Alessandra laughs happily as if nothing had happened and, once back on her feet, she takes hold of my hand. "Why don't all three of us go and celebrate together?" Erica is about to make a dirty joke but she stops and laughs, and we walk towards the city centre.

Barcelona is a city that welcomes you and adapts to your mood. Melancholic and welcoming in the first part of my trip, now it is brazened and festive, almost as if sharing our energies and emphasising the change.

In the club, a large group of Erica's friends join us. Spaniards, Londoners, Italians and Germans keep raising toasts in my honour and take turns to carry me around the club. I had no idea that Erica had such a big group of international friendships, nor that she spoke both English and Spanish so well. Alessandra is in ecstasy because she's got what she wanted and is celebrating with me, and because, with each toast, she's carried around in triumph too.

Reminiscences of her queenly nature that emerge harmlessly and which she happily gives in to.

Elena will be proud of me when I send her the video of the evening. Otherwise she would force me to organise another party to make up for the "old woman's birthday" as she had called it.

"Can't you sleep here with me?"

"No, my flight's tomorrow and my suitcase and documents are at my hotel." It had happened again, between one toast and another and a "come up to my room for a last drink",

142

Alessandra had given me my birthday present until four o'clock in the morning.

"Leave your room and come with me, so we can talk." "Every time you sound like that, we end up fighting, I'm not coming with you." She looks huffy but then she smiles "I've learned a lot from this trip. I love you and I want you but I know that we can't decide to build something by force. When all this is over, I won't be angry but we don't have to spell out every time, that there's nothing between us. Let's just enjoy things the way they are and then, when one of us meets someone or simply wants to stop, we can just say so. What do you think?"

"It was the same thing I was going to say to you but I wouldn't have been so clear and concise."

"OK babe, you're on." She lies on the bed and looks at me smiling "we'll see each other in Italy as soon as we have something interesting to do together." I smile too and, after giving her a kiss, I let my eyes run deliberately all over her body. "I'm sure we'll find something interesting to do on a regular basis."

One last kiss goodbye and I leave the room, feeling as if I've put some important pieces of my life in place, not because of the speech with Alessandra but because the whole trip has helped me understand things I've never really dwelt on. Erica, and the fact that she is so nice, is proof of this because, when I met her, I labelled her without even giving her a chance.

20

Elena eats huge amounts of food at an embarrassing speed. She always has and she never puts on weight, not even a pound, making all our friends and some of her ex-girlfriends angry and envious. We're having lunch at a Japanese restaurant and the stack of dishes to her right starts to lean disturbingly.

"You have to tell me everything you did, and I want all the details."

"This really isn't healthy you know. You should go and see a psychologist to try and find out why you have this need."

"You mean I should pay to have someone tell me that I've been secretly in love with you my whole life and that my masochism makes me want to hurt myself with juicy details?"

"Sorry, I still can't take my eyes off your new tits. Can't you feel the crumbs falling on them?" "Be serious! And no! I can't feel the crumbs."

"It's impossible to be serious with you. What I sorted out in Barcelona is much more important than the description of my recreational activities."

Elena listens to me while she eats some more. Her right cheek is full of food and her eyes pay attention to what I say while she uses her chopsticks to stabs a roll of seaweed and cucumber ready to put it in her mouth as soon as she creates the necessary space.

"Do you remember what I told you about the fortune-teller?" She nods as she leans interestedly towards me, chewing all the time, as if I'm whispering and she has to listen more closely. "When my mother died it was like I was frozen. I couldn't feel anything because it wasn't really my mother that was dead, but the woman who had killed her that famous summer when she accused me." At this point, Elena rests her chopsticks on the plate and concentrates on chewing what she has in her mouth. She wipes her lips with her napkin and takes a sip of water. "Maybe I need to pay more attention to what you're saying because I don't think I understand." "Do you remember what happened when we were twenty?"

"Of course I remember. You came back from that holiday devastated and stayed with me for six months. My dad was thinking of adopting you. That was when your mother started threatening to commit suicide every two months." "Exactly. From that moment on, my life got worse. She had always had problems and was never the loving mother most people imagine, but she tried to love me. In her own way she tried to impersonate the behaviour expected of a parent."

Elena squeezes my hand, knowing how difficult it is for me to deal with this subject, having gone through the pain with me when everything had happened.

"That summer she had forced us to go on holiday with her to meet her boyfriend of the moment, her first love, found again thanks to mutual friends. Neither my sister nor I wanted to go, but Emma still wasn't 18 at the time and I agreed to go so she wouldn't have to go on her own with my mother. One far from harmonious family going to meet another one." "But there was an upside to it all." Elena laughs, referring to Elio's daughter (Elio was my mother's partner at the time), who, as soon as we met, asked if we could sleep together to make friends. Sabrina, a girl the same age as me, with dreams of becoming an actress, and a complete awareness that she loved women. Since we understood each other at first glance, the holiday suddenly seemed to be much more interesting.

"And that was the problem." Elena looks confused "why do you say that? Your mother accused you of going to bed with Elio because she saw you climbing out of the window of their bungalow."

And from that day on, she made sure that my life was one long guilt trip because I'd been the cause of their break-up and

146

consequently the end of her life, the clinics, the antidepressants and the suicide attempts. And then of course she forgave me, despite the fact that I'd hurt her so badly, trapping me in a situation in which I was forced to feel guilty without having actually done anything to deserve it.

"When she asked me for an explanation, I told her that I'd been to bed with Sabrina and I've always thought she'd disbelieved me, until now. Now I realise that it's because she did believe me, but then immediately refused to accept the whole idea, that her brain created images in her head that confirmed her idea of me in bed with Elio." I shiver and make a sound of absolute disgust "and don't stand there pretending you're as pure as the driven snow because I know you've had plenty of men in the past" I say, laughing, as I remember our high school adventures. "If people keep telling you that you have to look for Prince Charming, then it's only natural to try to understand how come the feelings you have are nothing like the ones your friends all describe."

"But I don't get what you mean when you say that it isn't your mother that died but someone else." Elena always gets confused when our conversations become serious. She tends to get bored even when she's evidently interested.

"Because that's not exactly what I said. My mother died that summer and became the woman who decided she couldn't bear to have a lesbian daughter. As far as she was concerned, she'd done everything right and couldn't have been a bad mother. It was much easier to think that I was a slut capable of going to bed with her boyfriend than admitting that she'd brought up a monster. I continued fighting with her for years, even telling her she was mad, but for her to admit that I was innocent would have meant accepting that I preferred women to men. It would also have meant that I was right about the fact that she needed help, because everything she insisted she had seen had only ever taken place inside her head."

"So what pills did you take in Barcelona to finally reach this conclusion?

"None, it was Angelica and something Alessandra said."

"What do you mean?" Elena had had problems of her own with her dad and her interest seemed focused on investigating the possibility that she might succeed in finding a solution. "Well, since that day, apart from putting myself in situations where I've constantly had to justify my actions, every time someone has wanted something from me or expected me to behave in a certain way, all I've ever done is try to make them happy. It's as though, having accepted her forgiveness for something I never did, I mapped out my emotional and psychological future." If you allow someone to convince you that there's something wrong with you, even just the tiniest little thing, you end up believing it and behaving as a consequence.

"So now I feel free." It's true. At long last I can mourn the death of that mother who had her faults but whom I admired so much when I was a little girl, and whose approval I sought constantly. Now I know that I have to forgive myself for not having grown up sooner and having kept on trying to make everyone happy, apart from me.

"Sonia, the only way I'm going to forgive you for all this seriousness is if you pay for lunch and tonight's drinks too. And don't try wangling your way out of it because this has been the most boring lunch of my life and you should be feeling guilty as hell." She takes my hand and leans over to kiss my cheek. "I do love you. Anybody else would have just laid down and died if they'd had to go through what you have but you're just twisted enough to have found a way to come out smiling." Suddenly she gets up and grabs her bag. "Go and pay because you promised to introduce me to your friend Erica, and I hope she's as funny as you said!"

"It depends on her mood so don't expect a court jester!" "I hope she's in the right mood then because, after all your whining today, I could end up in the madhouse. Of course I'll tell everyone it's your fault and I'll try and commit suicide once a month, leaving a goodbye letter with your name in it, but my life, ruined because of you, will end with a horrendous accident, robbing you forever of the chance to make amends." She said it all in one breath and I was immediately overwhelmed with sadness, but just for a moment because she quickly added "have I gone too far or can we laugh now?" I love this girl and I could never be happy if we weren't friends. "We can laugh now!"

Erica should be here soon. We're going out for dinner and, at the last moment, she's decided to bring Lara, her first love, so I can meet her. A sort of foursome which will allow her to focus on Elena if they like each other or to escape with an excuse if they don't. I'm not particularly thrilled with the arrangement but Erica had strictly forbidden me from cancelling.

While Elena chats to Linda, doing her best to embarrass her with comments about the kiss she pretends she's forgotten all about, I think that Emma should seriously consider getting a new job, as she hangs up a sign on the door which says "we were open yesterday and no one came. This evening we can't be bothered. Try again tomorrow – we might be in a better mood." She pulls the shutter halfway down and suggests a party. "We're waiting for Erica and Lara but I don't know if they'll want to spend the evening here."

"I think it's a fantastic idea. I won't have to keep going outside for a cigarette." Erica pops up from under the lowered shutter, answering for everyone.

Elena turns around immediately, to get a first impression, and they both stand there weighing each other up.

"You're strange but interesting. I'm Elena, pleased to meet you." "I've been told that you judge people at first glance so does this mean there's hope? Erica, the pleasure's mine." They shake hands as someone, whom we presume is Lara, appears from under the shutter, hanging back a little to end a telephone call. A mass of black hair hanging loose onto a leather jacket. I've never seen anyone walk into a room backwards.

Elena smiles "that depends what you're hoping for but I think that, unless you make some severe mistakes, you should be OK." Erica turns to face me, laughing, "you were right, she's every bit as bitchy as you said she was."

"Yes, but I also told you she was gorgeous." Elena pulls a face at me just as the mysterious Lara finishes her conversation. Without realising it, she's drawn everyone's attention to her.

Even Emma, who rarely shows even the slightest interest in anyone, has been stopped in her tracks by this girl's unusual entrance. "Girls, this is Lara, my best friend." From the moment she turned around to come into the bar our eyes had locked and I noticed a sort of embarrassment which she hid immediately behind a broad smile. "Hi everyone. I'm sorry I'm late but I had a problem at work." And she begins telling us what had happened, describing even the tiniest details. I watch her, curiously, while she converses with Elena, who seems quite happy to listen. Erica walks over to me, smiling slightly "I'm glad you've met." "Why?" Elena glances across and winks from time to time, clowning around and finding the perfect sidekick in Lara who invades the bar with loud laughter. She doesn't just laugh with her voice but with her whole body, which moves energetically, as expressive as her face and words. It's as if she's full of dynamite and has to release it somehow so she doesn't explode. Lara is a concentrate of energy. "Because I knew you wouldn't be able to take your eyes off her." Erica puts her arm around my shoulders "your friend's beautiful but I don't think she likes me."

"Maybe I should have opened a hotel with themed rooms instead of a bar. Every time seems to be the right time for you to meet someone new. You all bore me to death. It's like watching an Argentinian soap but without men." Emma tells us that her friends are on their way "as long as your delicate lesbian balance isn't upset by a bit of testosterone."

"Emma are you sure you don't want to try going out with me? Because I think that you have the potential to be my other half!" Emma laughs, sincerely amused "Just keep trying Erica, one day it might just work."

Lara is on the phone again but this time she seems to be controlling her movements, to hide that same embarrassment I had noticed before.

Once Emma's friends arrive, Linda, struggling between distress and irritation, sets up the buffet and turns on the music. Lara talks very naturally to everyone, apart from me that is, because for some mysterious reason she hasn't even approached me yet. Since Erica's official introduction, we've not said a word to each other.

Hypnotised by her constantly moving lips, I can't help staring at her and, as if she's aware of the confusion she's creating in me, she keeps moving, moistening and twisting them. This expressive enrichment of her face reveals a clear attempt at feigning interest in and attention to a conversation that she really isn't following at all.

Erica continues eating her spaghetti with pesto sauce, looking happily aware of the fact that, from the moment she introduced me to Lara, it is as if my whole life has taken on a brand new meaning, merging into and becoming confused with a dimension that makes it impossible for me to do anything but keep looking at her, while desperately wanting to run as fast and as far as I can to one of those places created especially for hiding from the inevitable. I can feel her energy without even looking at her, which is probably for the best because, if I keep staring at her, I'm going to look like a manic psychopath.

"You're unusually quiet." "I'm not quiet Elena, I'm just eating." Even I can see that my plate is empty. I walk over to the buffet to get some roast potatoes, followed by both Erica and my best friend. "I hardly recognise you. She's gorgeous! Why don't you go and talk to her?" While Elena continues firing questions at me, Erica touches my forehead "maybe she's feverish" Emma joins us, impatient to get involved "maybe she's just not up to it. She's getting old you know."

Lara's nibbling at something, looking clearly and grumpily bored with the boy sitting in front of her, describing the interior of his beach house in minute detail. Occasionally she turns to look at me with those big catlike eyes which change colour from shades of gold to green in real time, keeping me hypnotised. As she fidgets in her chair, she answers him with questions that having nothing to do with what he's saying, and I wonder what her silence resting against mine would taste like. All I will ever remember about the evening are sensations, but virtually none of the conversation. I'll remember her eyes but not what I ate, nothing of what Erica and Elena are saying and nothing of what I am saying either.

I will remember the feeling of my life changing, along with the perception that I have already loved Lara in another dimension or time, and that I have found her this evening, not just met her, that I have spotted that little piece of the puzzle that was missing for years, making me feel a little grey and a little lonely, when, in theory, I had everything I needed to be happy and satisfied. My heart will always carry the awareness of that precise moment when I realised that I had fallen in love for the first time with a woman I had never seen before and who had to be the other half I didn't think I needed to look for.

It is as if we are wrapped in two skins that are slowly cracking, allowing our individual lights to filter through, inevitably flowing into each other after waiting a very long time. Feeling comfortable and not knowing how or why. But I'm terrified. Because if all this is the way my heart is reacting to what I have experienced in the last few weeks then it will be like getting back on that merry-go-round I've worked so hard to get off.

"So we almost ended up spending three days together in Barcelona." She walked up to me all of a sudden with a determined air and a steady gaze. "Yeah, but it turns out your job is constantly getting in your way." She smiles, investigating me with her eyes, as if she too is deciding how much to reveal about herself.

"I love my job and in actual fact it often saves me from embarrassing or devastating situations." "I don't think you can call a holiday devastating." "From what Erica told me, I'd have been bored out of my mind by the drama with your girlfriend." I need to remember to punch Erica in the face. "I don't have a girlfriend." Lara laughs noisily as she moves her hair to the other side of her head "does she know that?" Elena, pretending to look for something to eat, moves closer to eavesdrop and Lara slides over to make room for her. "Everybody here seems to be very interested in what we're doing, or is it just an impression?" Elena walks away, silently mouthing, with her mouth full, "sorry", heading off to report back to Emma and Erica who had sent her to find out what was going on.

Two muffled thuds on the closed shutter relieve the embarrassment, making everyone jump, apart from Emma, who shouts "we're closed" so loudly that she can probably be heard right down at the far end of the block. The thuds come again and then Linda, after exchanging glances with Emma, goes to let the new arrival in. Lara follows her, taking a position by her side, looking like a ninja with an attentive and watchful eye. She could be the star of an action movie but I can't decide whether to identify her with the goody or the baddy. Her body is coiled like a spring and ready to react. She seems to have already decided that something dangerous is going to come through that shutter and that she's going to have to exterminate it.

"Don't invite me when you organise a party." Alina smiles and says hello to Emma but her expression changes as soon as she realises that Erica's here, and she walks straight past her, ignoring her completely, to say hello to the other guests.

Lara walks back towards me, looking like she wants to kill someone. "Erica didn't tell me what you do for a living." She has decided to ignore Alina. This girl reveals her emotions without being able to disguise them at all, perhaps because she doesn't want to. "I am a photographer. I have my own studio and I work with a German company that commissions me to do all its Italian jobs. Do you know Alina?" She joins us with the precise aim of disturbing us. "Of course she knows me." She comes up to her and kisses her on the cheeks. "We met once at the club when Erica was cheating on me with someone and Lara was covering for her." I still don't understand whether Alina's annoying attitudes stem from real pain or from the sheer desire to mess things up. Lara smiles naively "sorry but I have a terrible memory. Do I really know you?" It seems like a clever way to stop someone in their tracks. Elena walks past me with a full plate and quickly whispers "I love her already". I hold back a laugh. "Ali, did you come here to be with friends or to wage war?" Her expression is icy: "What difference does it make to you? After four years together, instead of spending your birthday with me, you spent it with my ex!" Out of the corner of my eye I see Lara looking at me in amazement. Alina must have been talking to Alessandra. "I don't think Ale told you the exact version of the story. But it doesn't matter." Alina raises her glass and, also raising her voice so that everyone can hear her, proposes a toast: "to the woman who always has three versions of her life; the real one, the one she tells us about and the one we will never know."

"Shouldn't resentment be banned after eight years?" Elena fills the silence generated by the toast, causing an outburst of general laughter and enforcing the hatred that Alina has always felt towards her.

Lara, meanwhile, having joined Erica, is laughing with the others. Alina's bad mood has been swallowed up by the desire of the rest of the guests to party.

"How come you've managed to establish a relationship with everyone but not with me? Is there nothing about us worth keeping?" The evening is almost over and only a few of us are left. Emma's friends have gone and Linda's shift is over. Elena and Erica are chatting with Lara while Emma is deciding whether to stay with us or go home with Tito, who's been in love with her forever without any hope of overcoming the barrier between their sporadic friendship and the dream of being a couple. Alina seems sincere. "I can't stand your gratuitous nastiness, your blatant selfishness and the way you measure people by how useful they can be to you. Apart from that, there's nothing about our relationship that I regret. You've got a million good points." Alina refrains from starting an argument "so why don't we ever get together?" "Because you aren't willing to do the same with me or with Erica either. You highlight shortcomings, you demand respect and you won't forget the past. Until you find a way to accept that there are parts of me that you can't stand and parts that you love, there's no way we can have a relationship. She walks away without me being able to gauge her reaction. I watch her retrieve her bag and say goodbye to Emma. She walks over to the shutter and pulls it up to get out. "Does Alessandra know that you're only using her for sex or is she still convinced that you two have a future?" She says it on purpose because she's noticed the looks between Lara and me. Elena almost closes the door on her and turns around with her new breasts on show. "Shall we go to the club by the river and cleanse ourselves of all that negativity?"

"Are you bringing the buoys?" I couldn't resist.

"You deserve Alina and her nastiness!"

Erica joins Elena and, after kissing her on the neck, looks straight into her eyes and asks, "are you coming in the car with me?"

"Excellent idea. Sonia doesn't deserve my presence in her car anyway!"

"I'm going with Tito. I'll see you tomorrow." Emma had then exchanged a few brief words with Elena. Conspirators.

"I don't have a car, so I guess I'll have to leave you." Lara looks at me while the three directors of this performance all look at her. She knew that we had both fallen into a trap. "Oh no you don't! I've got a car. you can come with me."

"Erica is taking an incredibly long road to the river," my heart is beating out of my chest. "Yes, she often tends to take the long way if she needs to." She seems to be wheezing when she answers. Then she takes a deep breath and blurts out "can I ask you a question?" My phone rings just at the wrong moment and, since I'm holding it, Lara sees Erica's name on the display. "Answer it, maybe they've gone somewhere else."

"Yes!"

"I'm going to turn right at the fourth junction, while you're going to go left for two reasons: the first is that I want to be alone with Elena, the second is that you two are exactly the same but at different times. She's you before the trip to Barcelona with one difference."

Erica and Elena are dangerous together. "What's the difference?" Lara is completely absorbed or pretending to be completely absorbed in driving. "You give your whole heart while she never has, because she needs someone to love her completely with no masks and no lies." She hangs up and accelerates, so we lose her. "I knew she'd do that!" Annoyed, Lara tries to catch up with her, but gives up after a few blocks and slows down. "What were you going to ask before the phone rang?" She stops in front of a car park, pulls the handbrake and turns off the engine. "I had a weird feeling tonight. But before I talk about it, I need to know something." I feel like I'm perfectly in line with my life. I have a strange sense of what it should be like, a certainty that I've occasionally read about in books and have always attributed to the fruit of a narrative delirium, a legend that people like to believe in. I am certain that I have achieved something, and this is why I feel both happy and stupid, both excited and terrified. "What?" Lara smiles, "Are you the bitch everyone says you are? Because I am. So if we want to have fun there's no need to make a fuss about it, but I'm not and never will be second to anyone and since I don't know you well enough to trust you, you have to call the girl they call your girlfriend now and tell her that it's over. Otherwise, you'll never see me again." The impulse dictated by her ego makes me smile but the image of Angelica and Erica's words block my cutting reply. For the first time in my life, I can choose which path to take instead of just going with the flow. I don't need Lara to play the perfect girlfriend. I want Lara because I know she's perfect for me. And this knowledge is irrational and absolutely emotional. It's scary because she's asking me to be completely open, but since making peace with my demons, I've realised that opening up to love has nothing to do with reason, but with the thrill that runs through your soul and makes your body shake. A feeling that tells you the right thing to do, without a doubt. She still needs reassurance, security and tangible demonstrations to let herself go. Everyone has their own path and perhaps it is no coincidence that fate has brought us together today. I look at the clock. "It's 2 o'clock in the morning, a bit late to call." She seems disappointed but resolute. "It's up to you." I close my eyes for a moment, to listen to myself, to understand and to decide. As much as I want to get to know Lara, it's neither polite nor elegant to call someone at two in the morning. "I'll call her tomorrow morning and we can do whatever you want tonight." I see the disappointment in her eyes and the old me would have waived all my principles to erase it. "Don't think it's because I don't care. I don't have any problem calling her. I just don't think it's respectful to do it in the middle of the night." Lara laughs at me, "and you think everyone's waiting for you? She's probably fucking someone else." I'm smiling. She really is like me. "All the more reason to call in the morning. I wouldn't want to be disturbed if I were in her position."

We drive around and talk and, before we know it, it's morning. We take the hill road and wander around until dawn, talking about all kinds of things. The desire to touch each other is tangible but neither gives the other the opportunity to express it in any way. Lara parks her car at seven in the morning, in front of the ruins of an old aqueduct on one of the city's promontories. Setting out to explore like a child, she conceals a shared desire that is becoming increasingly urgent. I can't resist and I approach her from behind, wrapping my arms around her and burying my face between her neck and her hair. Her sigh generates a shock throughout my whole body, a feeling I've never experienced before that makes me sure of how I feel. Inclining her head slightly towards me, she offers me her lips, abandoning herself to a kiss that she has withheld on principle all night long but which she wants as much as me.

She turns to hold me and I know immediately that this entanglement is exactly what I need to live. Her eyes shine like mine are probably shining. "It's eight o'clock now. Do you think it's OK to call?" Stubborn and wary, she must think she has an advantage. "Yes, I do. It would be better to wait until nine, but I think I can make an exception."

Her voice is uneasy, as if she knows what's coming. "Why are you calling me so early?" But before I can answer she continues, "I had a terrible dream last night. You were on a boat with no oars on the rapids of a river and I was running next to you while the current was taking you away. You had a strange look in your eyes, as if despite knowing that it was you who was at the mercy of the current, you felt sorry for me. You told me not to worry and to keep the oars because you no longer needed them." Lara demands that I put her on speakerphone.

I have to make a choice. Being clear means hurting people sometimes. If I'm nice, I'll look like a fake. What do I want? "Ale, remember when we said that if we fell in love, we'd just say it?" Her silence is so cold.

"Yes."

"I've fallen in love"

"But I just saw you last week."

"I know."

"Maybe I'll forgive you some day." Lara didn't seem entirely satisfied, Alessandra wasn't at all and I, who had spent my whole life trying to please everyone, set out on my new journey making two people unhappy.

The air is cold even for November. Walking becomes really hard work, with Lara wanting to visit all the city centre shops, not to buy stuff but to discover clues, meet people and be amazed at things she hasn't seen before. I love this childish side of her that mostly torments me, forcing me every day to leave behind a sweet habit that she will never allow me to settle into. "There's a fortune teller staring at you, babe." She sounds like a conspirator. Looking in the direction that she's facing, I can't help but smile and I'm sure that Angelica is smiling too. Inside. I tighten my grip on Lara's hand and move closer as I shake my head in front of the final victory of the fortune teller who, with clear satisfaction expressed by her slightly raised right eyebrow, begins to shuffle the cards.

Standing in front of her table, I can't help noticing the same jam jar lid used as an ashtray and the same cloth that puffs up almost as if to say hello.

Lara looks from me to Angelica and back, probably waiting to be introduced, but I know that, after placing the deck of cards on the table, the fortune teller will speak.

"So this is her." She stares at Lara the way she had stared at me the year before and, in exactly the same way, Lara is captivated and hypnotised by her.

"Lara, I want to introduce you to Angelica, an old friend who taught me a lot during a trip we went on together that led me to you."

Angelica remains silent while Lara smiles.

"At last, the famous fortune teller! We've tried several times to find you, but never succeeded."

"Events depend on our actions so they follow a variable pattern. People meet when they're ready to understand each other." Angelica is more talkative than last time and less lapidary. "It took you a long time to be ready, girl! I thought you were smarter."

She's more communicative with Lara, but still cantankerous with me.

"I'm still convinced you need to improve your manners to increase customer loyalty." I'm joking because, being a romantic, I believe that there is much more than a professional relationship between me and Angelica. "You still tend to get lost behind your castles in the sky. You made peace with your memories last year, you aren't going to miss the present by pontificating about the alternatives, are you?"

Lara's thunderous laughter resonates throughout the gallery, making several passers-by turn around and, even though they're surprised, they can't help grinning.

"Babe! This woman is amazing. I'm always telling you that you think too much, too."

And, sniffing the air of the city where I grew up, I pull out the stool from under the table as Lara moves to stand behind me. I can feel her hands squeezing my shoulders. It's so nice to be so in tune that I can feel her excited curiosity from a simple touch. I don't need to ask or talk because I feel it inside, constantly.

"So Angelica, where are you taking me today?"

My old friend's expression seems softer and more indulgent, although I'm sure she won't be kind this time either.

"You're finally grounded. Let's see what the future holds for you." She pushes the cards closer to me, stares into my eyes and smiles as she lights a cigarette.

"Cut the pack."

Printed in Great Britain
by Amazon